ADVENTURE ISLAND

OF THE DIN... ..R DISCOVERY

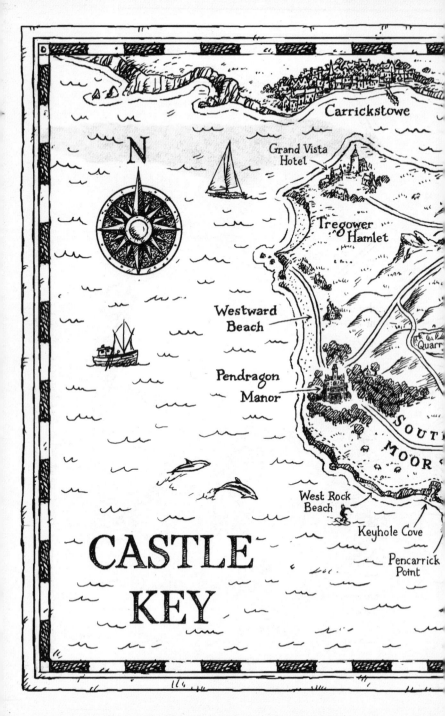

Carrickstowe

Grand Vista
Hotel

Tregower
Hamlet

Westward
Beach

Pendragon
Manor

Quarr

SOUTH
MOOR

West Rock
Beach

Keyhole Cove

Pencarrick
Point

CASTLE
KEY

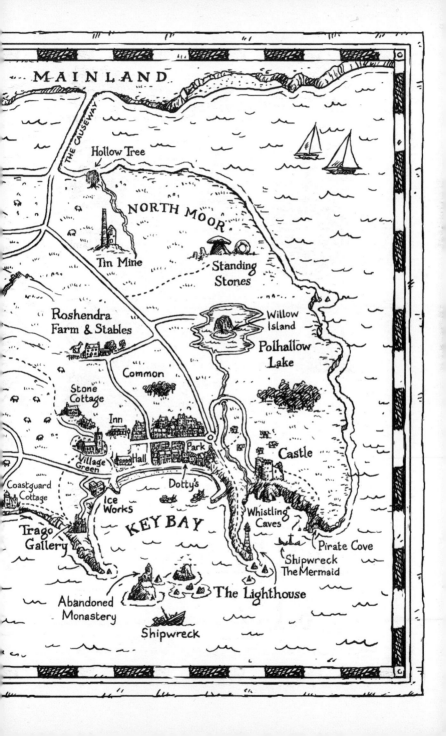

Collect all the Adventure Island *books*

ADVENTURE ISLAND

THE MYSTERY OF THE DINOSAUR DISCOVERY

Helen Moss

Illustrated by Leo Hartas

Orion
Children's Books

First published in Great Britain in 2012
by Orion Children's Books
a division of the Orion Publishing Group Ltd
Orion House
5 Upper St Martin's Lane
London WC2H 9EA
An Hachette UK company

1 3 5 7 9 10 8 6 4 2

A catalogue record for this book is
available from the British Library.

ISBN 978 1 4440 0533 2

Printed in Great Britain by Clays Ltd, St Ives plc

For Storm, Maia, Pip and Snowy,
the original Canine Division

One

Secret in the Snow

S cott stretched contentedly beneath the heavy, old-fashioned quilt. He'd had a long, tiring train journey from London yesterday. It had been almost midnight by the time the taxi from Carrickstowe station had crossed the narrow causeway and arrived at Aunt Kate's cottage on Castle Key island. And it *was* the Christmas holidays, after all. Yep, he *definitely* deserved a lie-in.

Suddenly something sprang out of the bed on the other side of the little attic room like a giant flea.

'Scott! You've got to see this!' the giant flea shouted at the top of its voice. Scott burrowed deeper under the quilt. Sometimes, if you ignored Jack, he'd go away eventually.

'This is awesome!'

Scott opened one eye. His brother was tugging back the curtains and peering out of the window. Scott didn't stir. Unless a horde of alien zombie death-beasts was sliming its way across Aunt Kate's rose beds, he just wasn't interested.

But now Jack was lurching about the room, pulling socks and sweatshirts on over his pyjamas. Scott tried to drift back off into that warm, sleepy place.

He was doing quite well until Jack body-slammed on top of him and bellowed in his ear. '*SNO-O-O-W!*'

There were some things even Scott couldn't sleep through.

—

Jack hurtled down the narrow staircase, taking the last four stairs in a single jump. He couldn't wait to tell Emily about the snow! Emily Wild – the boys' best friend on the island – lived in the old lighthouse on the promontory, which her parents ran as a Bed and Breakfast. On second thoughts, Emily had probably already noticed the cold white stuff falling from the sky. And on third thoughts, he definitely had to make a detour via the kitchen. Aunt Kate was frying bacon!

Jack sat on the counter next to the stove and munched on a bacon sandwich the size of a bread bin. This was the life! At home, Jack never had much to do in the week after Christmas, apart from consuming his body weight in chocolate and trying not to think about the homework lurking in his bag in the hall where he'd kicked it on the last day of term. So when Aunt Kate (who was *technically* his great-aunt as she was Dad's aunt really) had rung to invite him and Scott to spend the rest of the holiday in Castle Key, he had stuffed a toothbrush and a pair of jeans in a backpack within nanoseconds. Even Scott – who hadn't moved from his computer since receiving the new FIFA football game – had been happy to postpone Chelsea's bid for the Cup Final. Castle Key was *always* full of adventure – even in the week after Christmas!

And now there was snow too. It didn't get any better than this!

Jack threw on a random collection of hats, scarves and gloves and stepped outside. It was like walking into a giant Christmas card. Thick snow blanketed the grass, the path, every fencepost and every twig of every tree. Big fluffy flakes were still swirling softly in a pale grey sky.

'Fresh tracks!' Jack yelled, bursting to stamp the very

first footprints across the garden. Then he hesitated, one foot in the air. Someone had trashed his lovely snow already! A line of prints marched up from the garden gate to the front step. Who could have done such a thing? Jack looked more closely. There were smaller tracks too, as if an animal had been bounding around in the snow.

Suddenly a volley of snowballs bombarded him from behind the laurel bush next to the front door. The biggest snowball of all shook itself mid-air and turned out to be a flying dog.

'Drift!' Jack laughed, as a bundle of black, white and tan fur tried to lick his nose. 'Emily!' he shouted, as his friend popped up and fired off another round of snowballs. Her long brown curls streamed out from beneath a blue knitted hat and her black leather satchel was slung over a padded jacket.

'About time too!' Emily laughed. 'I practically got frostbite waiting for you to appear.'

Jack ran to join her. 'Quick! Reload! Scott'll be out any minute.'

'*Ambush!*' Emily laughed as she scooped up a fresh supply of snow and ducked behind the bush.

＊

After a marathon snowball fight the friends sat round a blazing fire in the living room, sipping hot chocolates oozing with marshmallows. Drift snoozed on the hearth rug, his fur gently steaming.

'Let's go sledging next,' Emily suggested.

Aunt Kate appeared with a tray of bread to toast over the fire. 'There are some old sledges in the garden shed you can take.' She smiled and tucked her flyaway white hair behind her ears. 'The last time those sledges came out was when your dad and Uncle Tim were here as boys. It hasn't snowed like this on the island for more than thirty years.'

Jack removed a thick slice of warm bread from the toasting fork, slathered on butter, jam and Nutella and took a bite. *Perfection!*

'We'll go up to the old quarry on South Moor,' Emily said.

'Cool! Quarry sledging sounds *extreme*!' Jack imagined himself bombing headfirst down a near-vertical cliff face.

Emily threw a cushion at him. 'Not *in* the quarry *obviously*. But there are some great long slopes nearby.'

Aunt Kate looked at the friends over her glasses, her eyes lingering for an extra beat on Jack. 'Yes, keep *well* away from the quarry. Last year some kids had to be rescued after falling into the water at the bottom. It's very dangerous!'

'Of course we'll be careful,' Scott promised. 'You know us.'

'That,' Aunt Kate muttered, 'is what I'm worried about.'

—

The friends dragged the wooden sledges to the top of Church Lane and along an old cart track, past a stand of dead hawthorn trees sculpted by the wind into the shape of three witches pointing their twisted fingers across the moor. Drift zig-zagged back and forth chasing snowballs.

By the time they'd climbed to the top of the highest hill they were all panting. The sun had broken through the cloud and the snow sparkled as if strewn with diamond dust. Emily paused for a moment to admire the view across the glistening island to the sapphire-blue sea beyond. But *only* for a moment. Then she gave her sledge a push and jumped on. At the last second, Drift hopped up to join her.

'Come on! It's a race!' she yelled as they flew off down the hill, Drift's ears – the black one and the white one with brown spots – flapping in her face.

Jack and Scott wasted no time in launching themselves after her.

'Awesome!' Jack laughed, as he crashed into Scott. 'I must have got up to fifty miles an hour there.'

'In your dreams!' Scott snorted.

They sped down the slope again and again, until at

last they flopped down in an exhausted heap. Long blue shadows were already beginning to slide across the snow.

Emily sat up. 'We should start back soon. It'll be dark by four.' She looked around for Drift. *That's odd,* she thought. *He was here a minute ago.* In the dwindling light she could make out a set of tracks disappearing into the distance. 'Drift!' she called. She followed the paw prints for a few paces and all at once, with a feeling of dread, she realized where they were leading. *The old quarry.*

Emily began to run, stumbling through the snow. She didn't stop until she came to a high chain-link fence. Her fingers clutching at the wire, she peered though the mesh. Cloaked in snow, the deep pits gouged into the hillside and the vast piles of waste rock looked more like a ski resort than a quarry. But the dangers of the sheer drops were still obvious, even without the KEEP OUT signs plastered all over the fence.

And Drift was still nowhere to be seen.

Emily leaned against the fence, feeling the cold wire press diamond shapes into her forehead. She pictured Drift falling from a precipice; plunging through a sheet of ice into the freezing water below . . . She closed her eyes to blot out the terrible image. Then she heard Scott and Jack calling her from further along the fence. 'Look! There's a gap here. Drift's tracks go through into the quarry!'

Emily forged her way through the snow towards the boys. 'I'm going in after him!' She knew it was dangerous and they'd promised Aunt Kate to stay away, but what choice did she have? Drift was in danger!

'I'm coming with you,' Jack said. He was already tugging at the wire to make the hole bigger.

Scott frowned. 'OK. But we stay near the fence.'

Emily slung aside her shoulder bag and wriggled through the gap, snow piling in at the neck and sleeves of her coat. She staggered to her feet as Scott and Jack squeezed through the fence behind her.

'Drift!' they shouted.

But there was no response. Emily began to run further into the quarry but Scott pulled her back.

'Are you *trying* to get yourself killed?' he demanded.

Emily was struggling out of Scott's grasp when she suddenly saw Jack point towards a heap of snow-covered rocks, not far from the fence.

'There he is!' he shouted.

Hardly daring to hope, Emily looked up. *Jack was right!* Drift was on top of the mound, digging so furiously he was almost hidden by a fountain of flying snow.

With tears of relief stinging her eyes, Emily ran to the little dog's side, dropped to her knees and pressed her face into his cold, wet fur. 'Never, ever do that to me again, you hear?' she mumbled.

Drift looked up, licked her nose, and gave the single

soft bark Emily recognized as *You might want to have a look at this.*

She examined the exposed patch of grey limestone where Drift's paws had scrabbled away snow and clumps of earth and grass. *There's probably a fox hiding under there,* she thought. But then she noticed several long narrow ridges protruding from the rock.

'Looks like some old bones,' Scott murmured, as he and Jack gathered round.

Jack cleared away more snow with his sleeve. 'Ooh, that bumpy part looks just like a spine!'

Suddenly Emily jumped back, pulling the boys with her. 'Don't touch! You'll contaminate the evidence.'

'What evidence?' Scott and Jack echoed in unison.

Emily stared at the boys, her dark eyes glowing with excitement. 'Well it's obvious, isn't it? We're looking at a *murder scene*!'

Two

Murder Scene

'Murder?' Scott gulped. He stared at his friend. Most people would be in shock if their dog had just dug up a murdered corpse. Or at least a bit *worried*. Not Emily. She looked as if she'd struck gold. He could almost see the thought-bubble over her head: *A new investigation! OPERATION QUARRY KILLING.*

'It must be some kind of gangland hit job,' Jack said excitedly. 'They've probably cut the hands off so the body can't be identified from fingerprints . . .'

Scott rolled his eyes. It was hard to take Jack seriously at the best of times. The fact that he was wearing a brown, fleecey lumberjack cap with earflaps that made him look like a giant teddy bear wasn't helping.

'The machines must have brought the body to the surface.' Emily pointed to a row of diggers and bulldozers parked nearby, like hibernating beasts under their blankets of snow.

Scott was puzzled. 'I thought this quarry closed down years ago.'

'It did. But they've started filling it in to make it safer. They're using these heaps of waste rock. The workmen told me all about it when I came up here to carry out some routine observations,' Emily explained, in a matter-of-fact tone – as if inspecting disused quarries was a perfectly normal holiday pastime. 'But they stopped work on Christmas Eve, of course, and now they can't work because of the snow.'

Scott exchanged a grin with Jack. Emily knew everything that happened on the island. Some people might call it nosiness. Emily preferred to call it 'intelligence gathering'.

Meanwhile, Emily had fetched her satchel from where she'd thrown it by the fence and was pulling out one object after another. 'Ruler,' she muttered. 'Magnifying glass, evidence bags . . . ah, here we are.' She grabbed a camera and thrust a torch into Jack's hand. 'Direct the beam onto the body while I get some shots. And hold the ruler up so we can record the size of the bones.'

The bones were the colour of toast, and had fused into a massive slab of rock the size of a minibus, lying on its side beneath the snow. Scott brushed away more snow and uncovered what looked like part of a skull.

Emily slapped his wrist. '*Murder scene!*' she reminded him.

'Except this *isn't* a murder,' Scott stated. 'Not unless the victim had horns, anyway. Look!' He took the torch from Jack and shone it onto a bony spike. 'There's no way this is a human skull.'

Jack groaned. 'What? You mean Drift's just dug up a bit of old roadkill?'

Emily looked down at the skull. Scott was right. There *were* horns. It was just some old animal skeleton. She kicked at the bones in frustration. She'd investigated all kinds of crime in the past – theft, kidnap, fraud, arson – but this would have been her first murder, and she'd been so looking forward to getting her teeth into it!

'There are strange bony plates coming out from the spine as well,' Scott pointed out.

Emily peered through the magnifying glass. The bones looked old. *Very* old. Up close, the texture was like the inside of a Crunchie bar. And now they'd cleared more snow she was starting to see just how enormous

21

the skeleton was. Suddenly she was interested again, even if this *wasn't* a murder case.

Scott sat back on his heels. 'Are you thinking what I'm thinking, Em?'

Suddenly Jack jumped up, his earflaps bobbing up and down. 'IT'S A DRAGON!' he shouted.

Scott shook his head very slowly. 'Yeah, right! Oh, look, there's a unicorn as well. And what's that? Ooh, it's a gruffalo!'

'I was *joking!* I know dragons aren't real,' Jack said, back-tracking as fast as he could and shoving Scott into a snowdrift for good measure.

But Emily wasn't listening to the boys' argument. 'I think,' she said, 'we've found a *dinosaur*!'

Three

A Visit to Coastguard Cottage

'Exactly!' Scott said. 'It's a dinosaur fossil. This could be a really important find.'

Wow! A dinosaur! Jack thought. *How cool is that?* But hang on! Was Scott just winding him up again?

'It could be a triceratops with those horns,' Scott said.

'Or a stegosaurus,' Emily suggested.

Jack grinned. It was clear Scott and Emily were deadly serious. They really *had* found a dinosaur.

Drift raised an ear and gave an uncertain yip at the sound of a dog howling in the distance.

Scott shuddered. He suddenly realized that he was freezing. Darkness was falling fast. 'We need to get home before someone sends out a search party,' he said. 'Let's mark the spot with a stick and come back in the morning for a proper look.'

Emily and Jack nodded reluctantly. Then, with a last glance back at the ancient bones, the friends hurried away across the moor.

—

'A dinosaur fossil, you say?' Aunt Kate asked, hanging the friends' wet coats on a clothes horse in front of the fire. 'How exciting. You should talk to Harry Atherton. He'll be able to identify it for you.'

Emily took a sip of her hot chocolate. She'd stopped with the boys at Stone Cottage to warm up before setting off home to The Lighthouse. 'Professor Atherton?' she asked. 'I thought he was an astronomer. He has an observatory on top of his house for looking at the stars, doesn't he?'

'That's right. But he's also been studying the geology of the island for years,' Aunt Kate explained. 'His sister Margaret is an old friend of mine. She looks after him. He's a brilliant man, but rather *difficult*. I'll give her a call.'

—

It was all arranged and first thing next morning the friends set off for the Atherton residence. Snow still lay thick on the ground as they trudged along the road to Coastguard Cottage, perched high on the rugged cliffs on the south coast of the island. In the old days, Emily explained on the way, the coastguard lived there to look out for smugglers mooring up in the tiny coves below.

'Sounds like the *perfect* place for you, Em!' Scott joked.

Emily laughed and stuck out her tongue at Scott, but she couldn't deny it. She dreamed of catching a gang of smugglers even more than solving a murder case.

The door of the old cottage was opened by an elderly woman in jeans and a fluffy black jumper. Her grey hair had been cut into a short wispy style and when she smiled her dark eyes twinkled. 'Ah, good! Kate said you'd be coming. I'm Margaret Atherton. I first met your great-aunt in Vietnam in 1969, you know.'

As they shook hands, Jack wondered briefly what Aunt Kate had been doing in Vietnam in 1969. Hadn't there been a war on there then? But Margaret was already ushering them into a dimly lit hall.

'Come in out of the cold. Harry will be down shortly. Silly old fool's had me running up and down all morning looking for some old star chart he's lost.'

As they entered, Jack tripped over Drift and almost fell headfirst into an enormous spherical basket by the front door.

Margaret Atherton turned and smiled. 'Superb, isn't it? It's for storing grain. Made by the Mundimba tribe of Angola.'

'It's very, er, nice,' Jack mumbled. *Never mind grain,* he thought. *It would make an awesome hiding place in a game of hide-and-seek!*

'Baskets are a window onto society, don't you think?' Margaret asked.

Jack had no idea what she was talking about, but Scott and Emily were nodding politely so he did the same.

'Sorry. You'll have to excuse me,' Margaret laughed. 'Baskets are my passion.' With a sweep of her arm she indicated the baskets stuffed onto shelves and hanging on hooks from floor to ceiling. 'I collect them from all over the world. Not in person any more,' she added, with a hint of sadness. 'Harry doesn't like to travel. But people send them to me.' With that, she led the way into an octagonal room. 'This was the coastguard's watchtower,' she explained. 'We had Harry's observatory built into it when we moved here.'

Jack craned his neck to look up. The tower was

topped by a glass dome, under which there was a circular gallery containing several enormous telescopes. The walls were lined with bookshelves, which could only be reached by narrow wooden stepladders. A woolly-mammoth skeleton stood on a plinth in the centre of the room.

'That's Ivan,' Margaret Atherton said with a smile. 'He was presented to Harry after a dig in Siberia years ago.'

Ivan the Terrible! Jack thought, eyeing the ferocious-looking tusks.

'What's going on down there?' A gruff voice boomed from the top of the tower. They all looked up to see a giant stair-lift spiralling its way down a metal structure that looked like a fireman's pole. As the stair-lift slowly whirred round to face them, the head of an old man came into view, growing straight out of the machinery.

Cool! Jack thought. But how come Emily hadn't mentioned that Professor Atherton was a mutant: half man, half robot? He stared, mesmerized. Then suddenly he realized, to his disappointment, that Atherton was not The Terminator after all. He was an ordinary old man with a bushy grey beard and small round glasses, sitting in a massive high-tech, electric wheelchair, customized with more gadgets than James Bond's car.

The wheelchair picked up speed and landed with

a mighty clunk. Then it shot across the room. Drift yelped and leaped out of the way.

'Gangway!' Atherton bellowed.

'Slow down,' Margaret scolded. 'You're a liability in that thing! Now, these are the young people who've found the fossil,' she went on. 'Kate Trelawney's great-nephews, and Emily Wild from The Lighthouse.'

Using his chin, Professor Atherton pressed a button on a control panel attached to the side of the wheelchair and spun round. 'Harry Atherton,' he boomed. 'Can't shake hands. Paralysed from the neck down. Freak diving accident. Cairo. 1988.'

Jack opened his mouth. Then he closed it again. There wasn't much you could say to that introduction. Even Emily was lost for words. But it seemed no response was needed. Harry Atherton continued without stopping for breath.

'In twelve days' time, it'll be perfect conditions for studying the Messerspitze comet. It only visits Earth every three hundred years. Been looking for my star calendar all morning. My sister hides my books, you know!'

Margaret snorted. 'You think I haven't got better things to do with my time?'

Atherton ignored her. 'No doubt my sister's been boring the pants off you with her infernal baskets?'

Scott grinned at Jack and Emily. Only a brother and sister could make winding each other up into such an art form! Scott knew how that worked. Jack was quite possibly the most annoying person in the solar system, but life would be very boring without him – not that Scott would ever admit it, of course!

'What's this about a fossil, then?' Professor Atherton barked.

Emily stepped forward. 'We found it near the quarry—'

'A little ammonite, no doubt!' Atherton cut her off mid-sentence. 'Or a shark tooth.'

'No, it's *huge*.' Jack stretched out his arms like an angler boasting about a fish he'd caught.

'The skull is one point five metres across,' Emily read out from her notebook.

'And it's got horns,' Scott added.

As they continued to describe their find, Atherton grew more and more animated. 'Could it really be . . .' he muttered. 'Surely not . . .'

'We've got photos,' Scott said.

Emily passed her camera to Margaret, who plugged it into a socket on Professor Atherton's control panel. An image appeared, projected onto a screen that flipped up from the arm of the wheelchair.

Atherton scrolled through the pictures with his chin-operated controls. When the slide show finished he flashed the friends a stern look. 'This isn't some kind of practical joke, is it?'

'No, of course not,' all three protested indignantly.

'I'll have to see this for myself. But you may just have found what I've been seeking for the last twenty years!' He paused to swallow, and when he spoke again his voice trembled with excitement. 'Maggie, fire up the beast. We're all going on a field trip.'

The Megamegalosaurus

T he 'beast' turned out to be a customized army Land
Rover. Reaching it involved Professor Atherton's
wheelchair whizzing along corridors, through
automatic doors and up an escalator that led directly to
the truck door and slotted Professor Atherton neatly
into the front passenger seat.

Although everything ran like clockwork, Atherton
could barely contain his impatience. 'Can't you get this

31

thing *moving*, Maggie?' he snapped, as Margaret fixed snow chains on the tyres. 'We'll *all* be fossils before we get there!'

At last they were on their way. Margaret coaxed the jeep down the steep coast road, terrifyingly close to the cliff edge, and then northwards over the snowbound moorland roads. When they pulled up near the quarry gates Emily cleared a porthole in the steamed up window and peered out.

'It's just inside the quarry on the mound.' Then she hesitated. The gates were fastened with several hefty padlocks, and there was no way they'd get Professor Atherton's wheelchair through the gap in the fence without rewriting the laws of physics. But before Emily could say anything, Margaret was revving the engine and striking out cross-country round the outside of the fence.

'There it is!' Scott cried, pointing to the stick that marked the fossil site.

'Hold on tight!' Margaret yanked down hard on the wheel, put her foot down and steered straight at the chain-link fence. 'Oops!' she said brightly, as they skidded to a halt. 'It's dreadfully tricky to stop on this snow. We seem to have knocked a section of fence down. Never mind, we'll prop it back up when we leave.'

Professor Atherton could hardly speak for laughing. 'Maggie! You really should work on your parking skills.'

Emily grinned at Scott and Jack. Margaret's entrance to the quarry wasn't exactly stylish, but it was certainly effective!

The friends clambered out of the jeep and helped Margaret drag Professor Atherton's wheelchair through the broken fence to the mound where Drift was already scrabbling to uncover his find from its shroud of fresh snow.

Atherton jabbed at his control panel and an extendable arm shot out from his wheelchair. A camera with a huge zoom lens telescoped from the end and moved around the fossil like a robot. Atherton examined the enlarged images through a special viewfinder that clicked into place in front of his right eye.

Emily could hardly bear the suspense. At last Professor Atherton looked up from the camera and spoke, his voice cracking with emotion. 'I need to run some tests to be sure, but this is almost certainly the new species of megalosaurus I've been hunting for!'

Megalosaurus? Jack thought he knew every kind of dinosaur there was; he'd seen *Jurassic Park* six times! But he'd never heard of a megalosaurus. Still, surely anything that had *mega* in its name had to be good. And big! 'Awesome!' he whistled.

'It certainly *is* awesome!' Atherton laughed. 'Megalosaurus was one of the first dinosaurs to be identified – fossil remains were discovered back in the nineteenth century. I started to believe they must have inhabited Castle Key island when I found fossilized footprints near Westward Beach almost twenty years ago. They matched the trail of megalosaurus footprints found near Oxford, only they were almost twice the size! And then there was the coprolite . . .'

'What's coprolite?' Emily asked.

'Fossilized dung,' Scott explained.

'Dinosaur poo?' Jack screwed up his nose. That was so gross it was cool! 'Eughh!'

'The coprolite fossils contained bone fragments from such large prey, they could only have come from a truly gigantic predator,' Atherton went on. 'I wrote up my findings in the science journals, and put forward the theory that a giant form of megalosaurus – maybe fifteen metres from head to tail – roamed Castle Key a hundred and eighty million years ago. But no one believed me. Nothing like this has ever been found in mainland Cornwall before, as the rock is too old. But this island has a unique geology – a band of Jurassic limestone – more like parts of Dorset . . .'

'That's enough,' Margaret Atherton told him. 'I'm sure they don't want one of your lectures!'

'Well, what are you waiting for then, Maggie?' Atherton snapped back. 'Take samples! Set up a protective cover! This area will have to be out of bounds until I've organized a full-scale excavation.'

'Wow! Our *own* new dinosaur species,' Jack breathed as Margaret showed the friends how to chip away tiny flakes of the fossil with a hammer and chisel and transfer them to a rack of small plastic containers. 'We'll be famous! So, what shall we call it? Scottosaurus sounds rubbish and Emilysaurus sounds like a girl group or something. What about Jackosaurus? That has a ring to it!'

Scott groaned and rolled his eyes. 'No one calls their discoveries after their *first* name.'

'How do you know?' Jack asked.

'Think about it! Have you heard of the mighty *Brian*osaurus Rex? Or the small but deadly *Sophie*raptor?'

'And anyway, Drift found it first,' Emily pointed out.

Scott grinned. 'That's right. We should call it Driftosaurus until it has an official name.'

Drift wagged his tail in approval.

'Dinosaurs are usually given Greek or Latin names that describe their appearance or behaviour,' Atherton explained. 'Megalosaurus means big lizard, for example. Then there's pachycephalosaurus. That means thick-headed lizard.'

Scott shot a look at Jack. 'Hmm, now who does that remind me of?'

Jack ignored him. 'So, if megalosaurus is big lizard, and this is the jumbo version, we should call it *mega*megalosaurus!'

Margaret laughed. But then she shot a stern look at her brother. 'Come on, let's get you out of the cold. I have enough trouble running around after you as it is, without double pneumonia into the bargain.' She turned the wheelchair and began dragging it back towards the jeep. 'This cold weather is so bad for his health,' Margaret told the friends as they helped with the chair. 'In fact, we were planning to move to Mexico this spring. The climate would do him the world of good. But if this fossil turns out to be the real thing, I'll never get him away from Castle Key now.' She sighed sadly. 'And I was so looking forward to Mexico. They have a remarkable basket-weaving culture there.'

Jack felt a bit sorry for Margaret, but his excitement soon took over again. 'I can't wait to text Josh and Ali and tell them I've discovered a whole new species of dinosaur,' he said. 'They'll be so-o-o-o jealous. In London we've never discovered *anything*! Well, apart from a dead fox on Mr Snelling's allotment.'

But Margaret Atherton shook her head. 'Let's keep this under wraps for now. We don't want the media making a big fuss about it until Harry's tests are complete.'

'Of course,' Emily replied. 'Confidentiality is of the utmost importance.'

Scott grinned at Jack. Emily made it sound as if she handled top-secret documents on a daily basis.

Jack laughed, but underneath he was cursing. Now he was going to have to wait to brag about his own personal dinosaur. And *waiting* had never been his strong point.

—

That night Emily sat up in bed in her room on the top floor of The Lighthouse reading *Survival Tips for Secret Agents: Volume Two* – her Christmas present from Scott and Jack. But she couldn't concentrate on *How To Treat a Scorpion Sting*, for thinking about the fossil. True, she'd been disappointed at first that the skeleton wasn't human, but a whole new dinosaur species was *almost* as good as a murder. And she loved having a really good secret to keep. She'd been training herself to withstand torture (in the form of foot-tickling) for years, just in case she ever fell into enemy hands and they tried to extract information from her. She almost wished someone would *try* to make her tell about Driftosaurus, just so she could put it to the test.

'And don't you go woofing about those dinosaur bones to any of your doggy friends,' Emily teased, ruffling Drift's fur.

Drift looked up hopefully from his post, curled up on Emily's knees. Did Emily say *bones*? He loved bones! He sighed and went back to sleep, most disappointed to find that none were in evidence.

Emily settled back down to *How to Remove a Poisoned Dart.*

She just hoped Scott and Jack could keep a secret too.

Five

Godzilla with Attitude

Scott and Jack were tucking into pancakes and bacon the next morning when Aunt Kate wandered into the kitchen carrying a mug of tea and a newspaper.

Scott stared at the front-page headline of *The Carrickstowe Times*: GIANT DINOSAUR ROAMED 'JURASSIC ISLAND'. He ran into the living room and switched on the miniscule television set. The local news was just finishing but he caught the words . . . *new dinosaur species discovered in Castle Key . . .*

'JACK BIG-MOUTH CARTER!' Scott yelled, hurtling back into the kitchen. 'You couldn't resist bragging to all your mates in London, could you? They've only gone and leaked the story to the press!'

Jack felt his face burn with outrage. 'It wasn't me!'

Scott glared at him. 'Yeah, right! You just couldn't keep it zipped, could you?'

'I bet *you're* the one who gave it away to all your stupid Facebook friends!' Jack yelled as he stormed out of the kitchen with a slam of the door. At least, it *would* have been a slam if it hadn't been for a doorstop in the shape of a large patchwork owl which meant that it ended up as more of a feeble *thwump*. Jack opened the door and booted the owl across the kitchen. Then he slammed the door again, this time with a satisfying crash.

He stomped up the stairs and threw himself on his bed. *Why do I get the blame for everything?* He was never going to speak to Scott again. He shivered and crawled under the quilt. The bedroom was freezing. Serve Scott right if he got frostbite!

He heard the doorbell ring and Emily's voice downstairs. *No doubt Emily thinks I'm a blabbermouth too.*

Jack stared at the cracks on the ceiling. *I've been up here for hours. I could starve to death for all they care. I'm going to have to chew off my own arm soon.* He glanced down at his arm. It didn't look appetizing. It was no good, he'd have to sneak downstairs and raid the fridge. He crept to the door and listened to check nobody was around. But at the exact moment Jack's right ear made contact with the wood, the door was pulled open. He tumbled out to find Scott, Emily and Drift lurking on the landing – spying on him to make sure he wasn't giving away any more of their precious secrets, no doubt!

Emily's expression was like thunder.

Uh oh! Prepare to be annihilated! Jack thought. But to his surprise, he didn't seem to be the one in the firing line.

'Go on! Say it!' Emily snapped at Scott.

'Er, sorry.' Scott squeezed the words out through gritted teeth.

'What's going on?' Jack asked suspiciously.

'I couldn't believe it when I saw the papers this morning,' Emily explained. 'So I called Neil Denton at *The Carrickstowe Times* to ask him where the dinosaur story came from.'

'And?' Jack demanded. 'What did he say?'

Scott made a sheepish face. 'It wasn't you.'

'Well, I told *you* that!'

'It was Professor Atherton,' Emily interrupted.

'*Atherton?* No way!'

'*Yes* way,' Emily said. 'Which is why Scott owes you an apology.'

Jack grinned. 'Oh, yeah. Actually, I didn't quite hear it properly the first time.'

'Sorry,' Scott mumbled.

Jack cupped his hand behind his ear. 'No, still not getting anything.'

'I'M SORRY I SAID YOU TOLD YOUR FRIENDS!' Scott shouted. 'Good enough for you?'

Jack savoured the moment. 'Hmm. *Nearly.* Just repeat after me. I, Scott Carter, admit I'm a total git and I don't deserve a brother as awesome as Jack.'

Scott punched Jack's shoulder. 'Don't push your luck!'

Jack decided to quit while he was ahead. He turned to Emily. 'But *why* did Atherton suddenly decide to go public? I thought we were meant to be keeping Driftosaurus all hush-hush?'

But Emily was already halfway down the stairs with Drift at her heels. 'That's what I want to know,' she called over her shoulder. 'Let's go and find out.'

—

The friends kicked off their snowy boots as Margaret Atherton welcomed them in. 'I know why you've come!' she said with an apologetic smile. 'The silly old fool couldn't resist bragging about his big find. *Just the local press*, he says. I told him to wait for the results, but Harry's so impatient. It's got him into trouble before. Come through. He's in his laboratory.'

Margaret led them along a corridor and into a large brightly lit room that had been built onto the side of the cottage. Display cabinets containing samples of rocks and fossils lined the walls. Low benches were covered with computers, microscopes, and other scientific instruments with flashing lights and whirring dials. Professor Atherton was in the corner, his gadget-encrusted wheelchair blending in with the other equipment.

'Excuse me, Professor Atherton?' Scott asked politely. 'But why did you tell the press about the dinosaur?'

'Yeah,' Jack chipped in. 'Because if it turns out to be an old warthog or something we'll all look like a right load of plonkers!'

Professor Atherton smiled. 'That won't happen. I've been running this program all night, comparing our fossil with all *known* species on the database.' With his chin he directed a laser pointer to one of the computer screens. Images of bones and teeth flashed up, each one rotating in all directions before being replaced by the next. 'So far there've been no matches.'

'But why didn't you wait until you'd *finished* your tests to go public?' Emily insisted.

Professor Atherton turned his wheelchair to face her. 'This is so important, we can't risk the quarry owners starting their safety work again and disturbing the site, so I decided to call the local press and alert the council last night.'

Well, that part makes sense, Scott figured. He knew from his dad's work as an archaeologist that building work often needed to be halted – sometimes for months – when there'd been an important find on a site, so that scientists could carry out a thorough investigation. 'Will you use carbon dating to see how old the fossil is?' he asked, remembering something he'd read in a science magazine.

'Carbon dating can only go back to about sixty thousand years,' Professor Atherton explained. 'We use radioactive elements with slower decay rates – like uranium – for something as old as this. Margaret has been busy preparing the samples for testing all morning.'

His words were interrupted by the sound of the doorbell.

As soon as Margaret had hurried off to answer it Professor Atherton whispered, 'Quick! Come and look at this. Maggie didn't want me to show you. Said it wouldn't be fair to get your hopes up, but what does she know?'

The friends gathered round excitedly as a horizontal screen shot out from the side of the wheelchair. A beam of ghoulish, green light projected upwards from the surface, gradually forming itself into a 3D hologram of a dinosaur rearing up on powerful hind legs. The monstrous jaws opened to reveal rows of enormous teeth, two fearsome horns jutted out from the top of its head and jagged spines ran down its back to the tip of its long, muscular tail.

'Computer model of what the new megalosaurus looked like, based on the bones we've seen so far,' Atherton said proudly. 'What do you think?'

'Wow! He looks like Godzilla with attitude!' Scott whistled.

'I'd put money on Driftosaurus to thrash a T-Rex in a fight any day,' Jack laughed.

Drift whimpered and hid behind Emily's legs. Emily picked him up and hugged him. 'Don't worry, it's not real!'

Professor Atherton hastily switched off the screen as they heard footsteps sounding along the corridor.

Margaret entered the lab accompanied by a woman wearing a smart camel-coloured coat, and a silk scarf draped over dark hair streaked with grey. Although she wasn't tall she walked with the upright posture of a retired ballerina. She was followed in turn by a plump young man with downy fair hair like a newly hatched chick. His raspberry red ski jacket was so puffy it could have doubled up as a bouncy castle.

Atherton blinked with surprise behind his glasses. 'Nadira! What an honour. You've come all the way from London to hear about our find.'

'Professor Khan is an old friend of Harry's,'

Margaret explained. 'She's a palaeontologist at London University. An expert in the late Jurassic era.'

Nadira Khan acknowledged the friends with a brief nod. Then she gestured towards The Raspberry, who was busy sneezing into a tissue. 'This is my research assistant, Melvin Spencer.'

'Incredibly exciting, isn't it?' Atherton enthused. 'A megalosaurus skeleton!'

Nadira Khan stared down her elegant nose at him, shaking her head slowly as if he were a disappointing pupil who really should know better. Then she turned to Scott, Jack and Emily. 'I'm afraid Professor Atherton has misled you. There is absolutely no possibility that this fossil is a megalosaurus. Large land-based dinosaurs simply did not live in this region.' She paused to adjust her headscarf. 'No doubt this will turn out to be a pile of bones someone has dumped in the quarry. Or an old animal skeleton. A big stag maybe, or . . .' she went on, glancing down at Professor Atherton, '. . . wasn't it a goat last time?'

Six

A Major Press Event

Emily's mind was a maelstrom of questions. Could it be true? Was their fabulous Driftosaurus really just an old goat? What did Professor Khan mean by *last time*? And if Atherton had got it wrong before, could he be mistaken again?'

Nadira Khan pointed at the computer, where bone and tooth matches were still cycling through on the screen. 'Nobody is going to take this find seriously,

Harry, unless you allow other scientists to conduct independent tests.'

Behind her, Melvin Spencer sniggered. 'Yeah, in a *proper* lab with a decent mass spectrometer. Not a Mickey Mouse operation with this kind of *antique*!' He sniffed in the direction of a machine that looked like a cross between a photocopier and a tumble dryer. 'And with a bunch of kids and dogs hanging around!'

Professor Atherton's bushy eyebrows shot up his forehead. 'So you want independent tests, do you, Nadira? Fine by me!'

Professor Khan eyed him warily. She'd clearly expected Atherton to put up more of a fight. 'And you'll give me free access to the site? I'll need samples of any igneous rock around the fossil to run uranium-dating tests.'

Atherton laughed. 'Be my guest. In fact, we'll take you up to the quarry now if you like.'

Melvin Spencer rolled his watery eyes. 'We can't visit the site in *these* conditions. It's snowing out there, and I have got a cold, you know.'

Professor Khan ignored her assistant. She pursed her lips and held Atherton's gaze as if she were planning her next move in a game of chess. 'OK,' she said finally. 'It's a deal!'

The conversation was interrupted by a loud knock. A skinny young man in white overalls put his head round the door and glanced nervously around the laboratory, as if expecting Frankenstein's monster to lurch out of the shadows. Emily recognized Liam Kerrow; he'd recently returned to Castle Key from a year at college in Bristol to help with the family window-cleaning business. She'd noted this purely as part of her routine observations, of course. It was nothing to do with the fact that he had the dark hair, denim-blue eyes and moody gaze of a guy in an aftershave advert. 'Sorry to bother you, Professor,' he mumbled. 'I wouldn't have let myself in, only the front door was wide open.'

Margaret slapped her palm to her forehead. 'I can't have shut it properly when I let Nadira in.'

'Why not just invite the burglars in for a cup of tea?' Atherton grumbled.

Liam shuffled and blew on his hands. 'Dad said to tell you we'll be packing up in a few minutes. We've got most of the snow off the dome, but that east wind's started up again. It's too dangerous for the ladders on the tower now. We'll come back in a couple of days.'

'Old Russ Kerrow's been cleaning the observatory windows for me for years,' Atherton remarked, when Liam had left. 'I wouldn't trust anyone else. Good to see he's training up the next generation.' Then he scooted towards the door. 'What are we waiting for? We're going on *another* field trip!'

Before they all headed for the Land Rover, Margaret set the security alarms on the laboratory and double-checked that all the doors and windows were locked – extra carefully after having left the door open earlier. Nadira Khan was worried her old blue Mini wouldn't make it over the snow-covered moorland roads, so she and Melvin Spencer crammed into the back of the jeep with Emily and Drift, while Scott and Jack perched on the jump seats with the equipment. They were halfway out of the garage, when a convoy of vans and cars screeched up the road and skidded to a halt on the drive. People piled out, some brandishing microphones, others lugging cameras and sound equipment. They all swarmed around Coastguard Cottage, ringing the bell and peering through the windows, with shouts of, 'Professor Atherton! Tell us about the dinosaur! Can we have a quote, please?'

'Looks like the paparazzi have caught up with us,' Jack laughed. He watched through the jeep window. Two reporters were even trying to snatch Russ Kerrow's ladder as he was loading it onto the back of his old red van. They must have been thinking of trying to reach upstairs windows, but Kerrow wasn't having any of it. He narrowed his deep-set eyes, tugged the ladder back with one hand and pushed the reporters away with the other.

'He's like Clint Eastwood in an old cowboy film!' Jack laughed. 'He didn't even stop to take the cigarette out of the corner of his mouth!'

'Never mind that!' Margaret slapped her hands down

on the steering wheel. 'Those idiot reporters have blocked us in! I'll get rid of them.'

'I've got a better idea,' Nadira Khan said. 'Let's invite them to come along. They can interview us at the fossil site together. Harry can explain his theory and I can explain why he's wrong.'

Professor Atherton agreed. 'Excellent! It'll be a major press event!'

Press event? That sounds fun, Jack thought. He pictured himself being photographed in a heroic 'rugged explorer' pose, pointing down at the fossil. It would be a double spread in all the Sunday magazines. If only he had one of those Indiana Jones hats and a big hunting knife to really look the part.

'*Hello!* I'm being crushed to death here,' Melvin Spencer sniffled, even though he and his puffy red jacket were hogging most of the back seat. 'Any chance we could get moving? Some time *today*?'

'Uh oh! Squashed Raspberry alert!' Jack whispered.

But Scott wasn't listening. He was pretty sure that Atherton was right about their find being a genuine new species of dinosaur, but he couldn't help thinking that giving a great big press conference before they knew for sure was just asking for trouble.

But it was too late to do anything about it now. The reporters had finally realized there was nobody at home and were now stampeding towards the Land Rover. Nadira Khan rolled down her window, leaned out and invited them to come along to the old quarry.

I've got a bad feeling about this, Scott thought. *If this fossil does turn out to be a dud we're going to look like the biggest lemons since those guys who claimed they'd seen Bigfoot driving down the freeway and it turned out to be a guy in a gorilla suit.*

Leaving the country and changing his name would be the only option!

Seven

The Hounds of Hell

Half an hour later, the Athertons, Professor Khan, Melvin Spencer, Emily, Jack, Scott and Drift were all gathered in a circle, staring down at the tarpaulin cover protecting the fossil, like mourners around a grave. A biting wind was whipping up clouds of snow all across the moor. It was so cold Jack wouldn't have been surprised to see a colony of penguins waddling over the horizon.

Cameras and microphones were trained on the little group from every angle. The last of the cameramen gave a thumbs-up. 'OK, we're good to go.'

'About time, too,' Melvin grumbled. He bent down and started rolling back the cover. 'Oh, who on earth rigged this up?' He tutted. 'What a mess!'

Professor Khan knelt to study the skeleton beneath.

This must be how it feels to be a film star, Jack thought. His instructions were to stand and watch, 'acting natural'. That was harder than it sounded. What *was* natural? He tried his Brad Pitt face and then his Johnny Depp face. Then he remembered he was wearing the lumberjack cap that Scott said made him look like a demented teddy bear. He quickly pulled it off and hid it behind his back.

Meanwhile Professor Khan was taking photographs of the fossil. 'It looks more convincing than I expected,' she admitted. 'But we'll see what the tests reveal. Melvin, could you start taking samples?'

The Raspberry sighed wearily and set to work chipping away flakes of fossil. 'Don't know why we're bothering. If this is a megalosaurus, I'm an orang-utan!' he muttered under his breath, as he picked up the tiny pieces with his tweezers and transferred them into plastic boxes.

Meanwhile, a journalist asked Emily to describe *exactly* how they'd found the fossil. Jack groaned to himself as she took her notebook out of her satchel. 'At approximately fifteen hundred hours on Friday . . .' she began.

We could be here for weeks now, Jack thought. And just when he figured it *had* to be his Indiana Jones moment, Professor Atherton started droning on about the 'enormous theoretical significance of the find'. This was even more boring than that three-hour tour of the sewage works in Year Six. He began to wander away from the crowd. Drift trotted after him – clearly fed up too. Jack threw him a snowball to chase.

'OY! WHAT'S GOING ON HERE?'

Jack spun around. Was there a law against throwing snowballs on Saturdays or something? But the security guard clanking open the quarry gates and puffing his way towards the mound seemed more interested in the reporters than in snowballs. Jack couldn't help grinning. Mr Angry might liven things up a bit! But his grin soon faded because the next things he saw were two black dogs, the size of panthers. And they were coming straight for him!

Jack stared at the massive snarling jaws. Strands of drool were flying out across the snow. He tried to turn and run for his life, but somehow his brain had lost all communication with his legs. He was fixed to the spot as the hounds of hell closed in on their prey.

'Agggghhh!' Jack screamed. He didn't want to be prey!

But just as he braced himself for the dogs' hot meaty

breath in his face and the tearing of their fangs in his flesh, the thundering of mighty paws stopped. Slowly Jack opened his eyes to see Drift bounding up to the two giant Dobermans, his tail waving like a ship's flag.

Jack watched in horror. Drift was now only millimetres from the hounds' slavering jaws. He was going to be eaten alive! Suddenly Jack was flying through the air, as if diving for a try in the last seconds of a rugby international. He reached to pull Drift away from the savage beasts but the little dog sprang from his grasp. Heart thumping, Jack prepared to leap into the fray once more. But then he stopped. What he was seeing – as much as he could see anything through a faceful of snow – was not the feeding frenzy he'd expected. The two Dobermans were bowing down and wagging their stumpy black tails so hard their whole bodies shook, while Drift scampered around, nudging their legs with his nose.

The dogs were playing!

Meanwhile the security guard had doubled over to catch his breath. In spite of the cold, sweat dripped down his face – which was the colour of a traffic light on *Stop.* He glared up at the crowd gathered around the fossil. 'What do you lot think you're doing?'

'Press conference, mate,' one of the reporters called out. 'About the dinosaur discovery.'

'*Alleged* dinosaur discovery,' Melvin Spencer corrected with a smirk.

'I'LL GIVE YOU DINOSAURS!' The guard roared. 'This is private property. And that,' he added, jabbing a finger in the direction of the fence, which had been breached by another of Margaret Atherton's minor parking failures, 'is criminal damage! Now scarper, or I'll set my dogs on you.'

All eyes flicked fearfully towards the Dobermans.

'Tyson! Rambo! ATTACK!' the guard screamed.

But Tyson and Rambo were too busy rolling around on their backs with Drift bouncing on top of them.

'Ooh yeah, we're *s-o-o-o* scared!' Scott whispered.

'Looks like Drift has made some new friends,' Emily giggled.

Suddenly Professor Atherton began to cough.

'Harry, you'll catch your death of cold!' Margaret snapped. 'We're going home this minute.' She tugged the wheelchair towards the Land Rover, deaf to her brother's protests.

The security guard began darting among the reporters like a sheepdog trying to herd an unruly flock away from the quarry. 'You heard the lady,' he barked. 'Nothing to see here. Move along now!'

The show was over.

~

'You'll all stay for lunch?' Harry Atherton asked as they arrived back at Coastguard Cottage, stopping his wheelchair with a 360° spin in the middle of the hall. He'd recovered from his coughing fit and was in high spirits again.

'Some hot soup to warm us all up,' Margaret offered.

'Best idea I've heard all day!' Jack said. Scott and Emily quickly agreed. It was a long time since breakfast.

Professor Khan checked her watch. 'That would be lovely, thanks. Then we'll head back to London.'

'Well, I'll have to visit the little boys' room if we're staying any longer,' Melvin moaned as if this were a major crisis.

Margaret pointed towards the tower room. 'Past the woolly mammoth and first on the left.'

Melvin stalked off, leaving his raspberry jacket and the case full of fossil samples in the corner by the front door – next to the huge round grain basket. *Made by the Mundimba tribe of Angola*, Jack remembered. *If only I could remember useless information like that at school, I'd be top of the class!*

'The kitchen's this way,' Margaret said, leading everyone through a door on the other side of the hall and down a short flight of stairs.

Mmm, soup. Jack pictured a huge bowl of chicken noodle, or minestrone . . . or cream of tomato with croutons . . .

'Luckily I made a batch yesterday to use up the Christmas leftovers!' Margaret hauled an enormous vat out of the fridge. 'Brussels sprout soup OK with everyone?'

Jack felt sick to the very pit of his empty stomach. *Brussels sprouts!* In his mind, he was staggering backwards, holding up his fingers in the sign of a cross. He'd managed to get through the whole of the festive season without a single sprout passing his lips – aided by sleight of hand and strategically placed paper napkins. But you couldn't hide soup in a napkin.

'Ooh, good! Give Jack plenty because he's *really* hungry!' Scott said.

I'm going to kill Scott for this, Jack thought, inching towards the table like a condemned man. Then, just when he thought there was no way out, Emily came to the rescue.

'I just remembered! Mum said I *had* to be home for lunch. And the boys were invited too. We'd better get going. You know what she's like if we're late.'

Jack vowed he would never, ever say this out loud, but at that precise second he thought he might just be in love with Emily Wild.

Mumbling their thanks and goodbyes, the friends backed out of the room. As they bolted up the stairs, they heard a muffled thud in the hall above them. Seconds later, Melvin Spencer elbowed past on his way down to the kitchen.

'Poor old Raspberry,' Emily giggled as they came out into the hall. 'Wait till he sees what's for lunch!

He'll really have something to complain about then!'

Jack laughed. 'Thanks for saving my life there, Em. I owe you one!' Hurrying across the hall, he noticed that the grain basket had toppled over again. Melvin must have knocked it down in his hurry to get to his delicious soup. *Odd,* Jack thought, as he propped the basket back up against the case of fossil samples. *What was The Raspberry doing over by the front door anyway? Had he got lost on his way from the loo to the kitchen?*

But Jack didn't have time to give it another thought; a whiff of Brussels sprout soup reached his nostrils. He raced out of the front door after Scott, Emily and Drift and gratefully gulped down a lungful of cold, fresh, sprout-free air.

Eight

Big News at Dotty's Tea Rooms

L ate next morning, Emily gazed gloomily out of one of the porthole windows in her bedroom. The sky was the muddy yellow of an old bruise. Battleship-grey waves crashed against the rocks far below. Even the seagulls looked cold. Finding Driftosaurus had been so exciting, but now all they could do was wait for the results of the scientists' tests to prove he was really a giant megalosaurus. 'If only we had a *proper*

investigation to work on,' she sighed, belly-flopping onto her bed. Drift opened one eye and then continued snoring softly.

Emily reached for her phone and rang the boys at Stone Cottage. They were at a loose end too. They'd spent the morning playing old board games from Aunt Kate's cupboard, Scott reported. But there were only so many times you could play Operation without having a nervous breakdown. 'Especially because Jack cheats all the time,' he laughed. 'And now he says playing Hungry Hippos has made him ravenous.'

'Let's meet at Dotty's for lunch,' Emily suggested. Suddenly she jumped to her feet. 'Ooh, you've not been to Dotty's yet this holiday, have you? Wait till you see what's new!'

Scott couldn't help feeling curious as he and Jack hurried along the seafront.

Dotty's Tea Rooms was a traditional seaside café that specialized in fish and chips and cream teas. It wasn't exactly a high-fashion celebrity dining experience. What could this revolutionary new feature be? Curry flavoured Cornish pasties? Deep fried scones?

'Don't tell me,' Jack said. 'Dotty's started serving the ketchup in those little sachets instead of bottles. I can't stand sachets. The sauce squirts everywhere when you open them.'

'You *really* need to get out more!' Scott teased.

'Hang on. Is that *pizza* I can smell?' Jack asked.

'Only the best pizza this side of Rome!' Emily laughed, running to join them from the other direction.

The small café, with its red checked tablecloths and paintings by local artists on the walls, was warm and steamy and very busy. In the far corner, Dotty was pulling pizzas out of a brand new wood-fired oven with a long-handled paddle. She looked up and waved to the friends as they found a table.

Jack pulled off his coat and grabbed the menu. 'I'll have the Castle Key Special with extra pepperoni, mushrooms, chilli and mozzarella,' he sighed happily.

'Hey, it's the famous Castle Key dinosaur hunters!'

The voice came from the table behind them. There was a roar of friendly laughter. Scott recognized Old Bob and several other fishermen, along with Pete Morley, a builder the friends had met during Operation Treasure, and Russ Kerrow, the window-cleaner.

'Lucky you found it before they sent the bulldozers in!' one of the fishermen commented.

'That's right!' Pete Morley chuckled. 'They'll be starting work on Camelot World, or whatever it's called, soon.'

'Camelot World?' Scott echoed.

'Yeah, they're going to build a King Arthur theme

park up on the quarry site,' Pete replied. 'A sort of medieval Disneyland. Knights and jousting and banquets and all that.'

'Cool!' Jack whistled. 'I hope they have some good rides.'

'*Not* cool!' Emily snapped. 'It'd take over the whole island. Anyway, it's just a silly rumour.'

Old Bob nodded. 'That's right. They'd never get planning permission to put a monstrosity like that on Castle Key.'

'Let's hope not,' Kerrow agreed, a frown deepening the lines in his weather-beaten face. 'We don't want all that hullaballoo here.'

'It *would* bring jobs to the island though,' Pete Morley pointed out. 'I heard they're building a big hotel complex and everything.'

Kerrow stirred his tea. 'You sound like my Liam. He keeps on about how we should try to get the contract for cleaning all the hotel windows. We'd make a fortune, he says!'

The conversation was put on hold as the pizzas arrived. Jack fed a piece of crust to Drift under the table. Then he wafted a huge slice under his nose, sniffing its aroma like a professional wine taster. He closed his eyes and nodded slowly. 'Oh, yeah. I've discovered an entirely new species of pizza. I shall name it Megamegapizzasaurus.'

Everyone laughed.

After a few moments of serious eating, Scott took a slurp of his Coke. 'So this story about a theme park at the quarry is definitely just a rumour then, Em?'

Emily propped her chin on her elbows. 'I hope so. Mum and Dad have started up this protest group of local business people to fight it, just in case. They're called HOCKI.'

'What's hockey got to do with it?' Jack asked.

Emily laughed. 'HOCKI stands for Hands Off Castle Key Island. I've done some background research for them. There *was* this guy, Charlie Raven, from a big property company in Bristol called Raven Resorts, sniffing around a few months ago. Raven Resorts are pretty dodgy from what I can tell; they've been in trouble for not having the proper safety standards. But I haven't been able to find any hard evidence that they're planning to build on the quarry, or even that they've bought the land.'

Scott relaxed. *Nothing* happened on Castle Key without Emily knowing about it. It wasn't that he didn't *like* theme parks – they were great – but it would swamp the tiny island, which now felt like his home just as much as London did. 'Probably just scaremongering by people like Mrs Loveday,' he suggested. 'You know how she's got a thing against mainlanders and their Big City Ways.'

Jack grinned. Mrs Loveday – Castle Key's Chief Busybody – was his arch-enemy. 'Now, I'm not one for tittle-tattle,' Jack squawked, imitating Mrs Loveday's favourite phrase. 'But I was in the post office and the vicar's sister's cousin's hairdresser told me . . .' Jack broke off, suddenly noticing that Scott and Emily were staring over his shoulder towards the door.

'Shh! Don't look now,' Scott hissed, 'but Mrs Loveday just walked in!'

'Yeah, right!' Jack laughed. 'Like I'm going to fall for that one!' He had his back to the door but he knew Scott was just having him on. '. . . so I said to my Norman,' he continued, 'if they think I'm having the Knights of the Round Table in my back garden, then my name's not Irene Loveday!'

Jack's voice rang out in the silence. He hesitated. Why had everyone else stopped talking? His heart sank like cold custard as he turned in his chair to see a familiar hunched figure standing in the doorway. Instead of her usual cycle helmet, she had a bright pink bobble hat pulled down over her grey curls. Jack tried to hide his caught-in-the-act expression by taking a big bite of pizza. *Then* he tried to ignore the searing pain of molten cheese welding itself to the roof of his mouth. It was no good! White-hot mozzarella sprayed across the café.

Amazingly, Mrs Loveday barely seemed to notice Jack's unusual greeting. 'They're swarming all over the island,' she wailed. 'It's an invasion!'

Swarming? Invasion? Scott stared at the old lady, his

66

mind reeling with images of Martian spaceships and killer bees.

'Hippies!' Mrs Loveday cried. 'They're setting up one of those peace camps on the common. It'll be all loud music and free love.'

'Hey, where can I get a ticket?' Pete Morley joked.

Mrs Loveday glared at him. 'You may scoff but you'll be sorry when your kids are being Boil Washed into one of those loony religious cults . . .'

'Do you think she means *brain*washed?' Emily whispered.

Mrs Loveday settled down at the counter and began chatting to Dotty while the friends turned back to their pizzas. But a few minutes later, Scott almost choked on an olive when a voice cackled in his ear, 'Steer clear of those drug-crazed hippies, won't you? They'll all be Smoking Cannibals, you mark my words!'

Scott was usually the best of the friends at keeping a straight face when Mrs Loveday came out with one of her mix-ups, but this time he was caught out by the element of surprise. Laughter began to bubble up in his chest like molten lava.

'Do you mean *cannabis*?' Emily asked politely.

'That's what I said, dear,' Mrs Loveday huffed. 'They'll all be On Their Heads!'

'Or *off* their heads, even!' Jack whispered.

It was no good! Scott caught Jack's eye and the volcano erupted. For the first – and he hoped, last –

time in his life, he laughed so hard he actually fell off his chair.

Emily jumped up, grabbed her coat and Scott's shoulder. 'Come on. Let's get you out of here!'

'Don't worry, he's just having one of his funny turns!' Jack mouthed in a loud stage whisper as he followed them out through the crowded café. 'Must be a full moon tonight!'

This could just be the high point of my life! Jack thought. Scott I'm-so-cool-I'm-in-danger-of-giving-myself-frostbite Carter had made a total wally of himself in a public place. It didn't get much better than that!

'A peace camp full of cannibals?' Emily giggled, as she propped the still-spluttering Scott against the harbour wall.

'And Mrs Loveday thinks we're going to steer clear?' Jack laughed. 'Come on. What are we waiting for?'

Nine

Ancient Dragons and Alien Lizards

To Jack's disappointment, there were no cannibals on the common. Only a beat-up purple camper van parked under the chestnut trees. There was no loud music either, but a young woman was sitting by a campfire playing a lute and making a wailing noise that Jack could only guess was singing of some kind. She wore a long green cloak round her shoulders fastened with a clasp in the shape of a Celtic knot. She looked up from beneath a mass of blonde dreadlocks, smiled and gestured that the friends were welcome to join her. They sat down on upturned logs around the fire-pit, holding out their hands to the flames, while Drift stretched out to toast his tummy.

A second woman – tall and pretty with very dark skin and ribbons twisted through her long black hair – stepped out of the van and joined them at the fire. She was wearing so many jumpers and cardigans over her long velvet dress that she looked like a human pass-the-parcel. She showed no hint of surprise that three strangers and a dog had suddenly materialized around the fire.

'My name is Izzy,' Lute-Woman trilled in a high, soft voice, still strumming away. 'And this is Skye.'

'So what brings you to Castle Key?' Emily asked, once the friends had introduced themselves. 'Are you staying long?'

Jack grinned. Emily's idea of polite conversation could often be mistaken for a police interrogation.

But Izzy didn't seem to mind. 'We've come to see the ancient dragon.'

Jack frowned. 'Sorry. Did you say *dragon*?'

'You know! The "dinosaur" fossil?' Skye drew air quotes with her fingers around the word *dinosaur*. 'It *proves* that Castle Key is the last remaining fragment of the lost island of Lyonesse, home of brave Tristan, the dragon-slayer . . .'

Now Jack had really lost the plot. This was worse than double history on a Friday afternoon when you dozed off for five minutes and woke to find the teacher had moved on from Ancient Egypt to World War Two. 'How do you "lose" an island?' he asked. 'And who's this Tristan bloke, anyway?'

Emily laughed. 'They're talking about the legends of King Arthur. Tristan was a Knight of the Round Table. He came from Lyonesse, which was a magical kingdom off the coast of Cornwall – until it disappeared beneath the waves.'

'I hope he was a good swimmer then,' Jack muttered.

'Let me get this straight,' Scott interrupted. 'You think the fossilized bones we found belonged to a *dragon*?'

Izzy smiled sweetly. 'What other logical explanation could there possibly be?'

Scott shook his head. He could think of several, and none of them involved fire-breathing mythical creatures. 'Sorry, but Professor Atherton says the dinosaur is over a hundred million years old. There weren't even cavemen around then, let alone knights.'

'That's right. The timing really doesn't work,' Emily said, seriously, as if investigating a simple burglary.

Skye sat down and stroked Drift's ears. 'Dragons can live for thousands of years,' she pointed out in a matter of fact tone.

Hang on a minute, Scott thought. *No one can* really *be this bonkers, can they?* Of course! How could he have been so stupid? It *had* to be a set-up! Maybe some kind of mad publicity stunt for that King Arthur theme park Pete Morley was talking about. *And I walked right into it!* Scott jumped up and looked round, expecting a film crew to step out from behind the trees. Then he glared down at Izzy and Skye. 'OK! You can drop the act now. Where are the cameras?'

Izzy's face crumpled as if Scott had accused her of being a serial puppy-strangler.

'I don't know what you mean,' Skye quavered. Drift licked her hand as if to reassure her that at least *he* believed her.

Suddenly Scott felt like a total scumball. It was obvious Izzy and Skye were telling the truth – or, at least, their own special version of the truth.

'Just ignore my brother,' Jack said sweetly. 'He can't help it. He has these delusions that people are filming him all the time.'

Skye gave Scott a sympathetic smile. 'Oh, yes, I've had that. Try camomile tea. It's very soothing.'

'If you want to see the, er, dragon, we can show you where it is,' Scott offered, trying to make up for his blunder.

Izzy smiled. 'We'll go to the standing stones at dawn to consult our spirit guides about the most favourable day to visit.'

Meanwhile Skye had lifted the lid from a big pot hanging over the fire and was stirring the contents. A sour cabbagey smell wafted out. 'Will you stay and eat with us? There's plenty.'

Jack watched in horror as green slime dripped from the wooden spoon.

'It's Brussels sprout stew,' Skye announced proudly. 'They were selling the sprouts off half-price in Carrickstowe market.'

Jack couldn't believe it. Brussels sprouts were hunting him down wherever he went. What did they want? *Revenge?* 'Er, bit full. Just eaten,' he blurted, scrambling to his feet and backing away from the fire.

Izzy played a few notes on her lute. 'We're expecting loads more friends to arrive soon. They're all really excited about the dragon. We'll be having a sing-song. You can stay and join in if you like.'

Now it was Scott's turn to make a sharp exit. 'Another time, maybe.' He'd rather cut off his ears than listen to any more of Izzy's singing!

'See! Told you it was a dragon!' Jack whispered, as they hurried away across the common. For a moment, he saw himself, head to toe in armour, smiting off a dragon's head with a glittering sword. *Smite! Smite!* He loved that word! He didn't much fancy being called *Tristan*, though.

'Repeat after me!' Scott said firmly. 'There are no such things as dragons!'

It seemed Skye and Izzy weren't the only visitors drawn to Castle Key by the dinosaur discovery. The friends drifted back to The Lighthouse to see if there was a good film to watch on TV, only to find that the guest lounge on the ground floor had been taken over by three men and a woman, who were lounging on the sofas, surrounded by piles of cases and crates. It looked as if they were planning either a film shoot or a military operation.

'Our new guests,' Emily's dad explained, as he came in with a tray of drinks. 'They're very interested in the fossil. I was telling them how you were the ones who found it.'

A tall spindly man unfolded himself from the sofa and stood up to shake hands. 'Graham Fothergill,' he announced, his eyes magnified behind thick glasses with square black frames. 'Congratulations on a phenomenal find!'

'Cheers!' Jack said, trying not to stare at Graham's unusual choice of headgear: a hat crafted from layers of tin foil.

Graham noticed his interest. 'Keeps out the radio waves. Can't be too careful!'

'Right,' Jack mumbled.

'You don't think that the dinosaur fossil is a dragon, by any chance, do you?' Scott asked.

An older man – who looked uncannily like an overgrown garden gnome – glanced up from unpacking a satellite dish from a metal box. 'A dragon? Nonsense! You've been reading too much Harry Potter!'

Emily laughed. 'That's a relief.'

The woman – who was dressed in dungarees and a brown checked shirt – introduced herself as Molly Dunnock. 'We're here to run scientific tests,' she said enthusiastically, her ponytail of springy, copper hair bobbing up and down as she spoke. 'We're looking for electromagnetic signals that only occur in objects from outer space. We should be able to prove beyond doubt that these fossil remains belong to one of the extraterrestrials that have been visiting our planet for millennia . . .'

The plump man sitting next to her held up something that looked like a television aerial and examined it seriously. 'The aliens are reptilian – a bit like giant lizards. But they can take on other forms to blend in on the host planet, of course . . .' He took a slurp of his Coke.

Jack, Scott and Emily stared at each other in disbelief. Had they just wandered into an episode of *Dr Who*?

'Right, we'll, er, leave you guys to it, then,' Emily mumbled, backing away, pulling Scott and Jack with her. They hurtled up the spiral staircase, burst into Emily's room and all fell on the bed helpless with laughter.

'Aliens!' Emily gasped.

'*Giant lizard* aliens!' Scott corrected.

'*Shape-shifting* giant lizard aliens!' Jack gasped through howls of laughter. These guys made Izzy and Skye and their dragon look positively *normal*!

—

Over the next two days, people continued to flock to the island to see Driftosaurus. Mrs Loveday went into gossip meltdown, especially when she spotted Izzy and Skye and their friends dancing around the standing stones on North Moor on her way to an early-morning cleaning job in Tregower. But apart from building battalions of snow-dragons versus snow-lizards on the common, Scott, Jack and Emily found themselves with little to do.

But then, on Tuesday morning, Margaret Atherton phoned. Would they come to Coastguard Cottage straight away? she asked; her brother was most anxious to see them.

Harry Atherton had just received a call from Nadira Khan in London.

Ten

Prime Suspect

'*Most anxious to see us?' What does that mean?*
Emily wondered as they raced up the drive to
Coastguard Cottage. Maybe Professor Atherton had
some good news about their dinosaur. But, deep down,
she knew that *anxious* was not a 'good news' kind of
word.

And she was right. When Harry Atherton met them
in the tower room he seemed to have shrunk inside

his wheelchair. And it was soon clear why. 'Nadira Khan phoned from London this morning,' he said in a mumble that was only a shadow of his usual booming voice. 'Her tests all show that the fossil samples are only ten thousand years old. Your find could be some kind of prehistoric mammal, but it's not old enough to be a dinosaur of any kind.'

Emily stared blankly at Scott and Jack. None of them could hide their disappointment. Even Drift's ears drooped. Their fantastic fossil was a boring old *mammal*? And seeing the despair etched onto Professor Atherton's face just made it worse.

Emily knelt and held the old man's hand, propped lifelessly against the arm of the wheelchair. 'A mammal could still be interesting, couldn't it?' she said, trying to look on the bright side.

'Yes, Emily's right,' Scott said bravely. 'It could be a sabre-tooth tiger or a cave bear?'

'Or a dragon!' Jack ventured.

Professor Atherton shook his head sadly. 'There's something else, I'm afraid. Nadira says she's found all kinds of contamination in the samples – traces of odd chemicals – she's convinced the fossil was *planted* . . .'

'*Planted*?' Emily gasped. 'You mean it's a . . .'

'. . . a hoax.' Professor Atherton's voice faded to a whisper as he finished her sentence for her. 'Yes. That's what it looks like.'

An hour later and Jack was so still so shell-shocked by Professor Atherton's news that he barely noticed when Dotty set his pizza down in front of him. 'A hoax?' he repeated, for the gazillionth time. 'I don't believe it!'

Scott frowned into his hot chocolate. For once he agreed with Jack. 'How *can* it be a hoax? The bones are fused right into the rock. The "hoaxers" would have to have driven over the moor with that massive slab of limestone in a whopping great truck!'

'You'd think someone might have *noticed*!' Jack snorted.

'Hmmm,' Emily mused. 'I guess it *could* have been one of the workmen that have been making the quarry safe. They're always hauling rocks about on trucks, so nobody would think that was odd. And any tyre tracks up to the mound would have been hidden by the snow . . .'

Scott wasn't convinced. 'But if it was a hoax, how come Professor Atherton's tests haven't been showing all those odd chemicals that Professor Khan was on about?'

Emily nodded. She'd been asking herself exactly the same thing.

But it was a different question that was bothering Jack. In his long career as School Joker he'd planted many a hoax object, ranging from the simple but effective box of rubber eggs in a cookery lesson, to the more elaborate hand-crafted wasps' nest in the girls' changing room. 'Anyone knows that the whole *point* of a hoax is for it to be *found*,' he said. 'You don't lug a massive great boulder across a remote moor and dump it in the middle of nowhere in the vague hope some kids *might* go sledging nearby and their dog *might* just wander off and start digging it up! Not unless you're seriously stupid,' he concluded.

Emily fed the last of her pizza to Drift. 'Jack's right. A hoax makes no sense. All the evidence points to one conclusion: the fossil we found is *not* a hoax, but someone wants the world to *think* it is.'

Jack stroked his chin and pretended to be straining his brain. 'Ooh, that's a difficult one! Would that someone's initials be N. K., I wonder?'

'Nadira Khan *is* the obvious suspect,' Emily agreed.

'The *only* suspect, you mean,' Jack corrected. 'What are we waiting for? Let's call Detective Inspector Hassan.'

Scott held up both hands. 'Whoah! We can't accuse her before we've got any evidence. What if we're wrong? We don't want to do an Atherton and go public before we've checked all our facts.'

Emily took out her notebook and pen. 'I think,' she said, her dark eyes glowing with excitement, 'we've finally got ourselves a new investigation.' She turned to a blank page, wrote *OPERATION DINOSAUR* and underlined it twice. 'So, we've already got our prime suspect. We know Khan had the opportunity, of course. All she had to do was switch the *genuine* fossil samples she took with other bits of bone she had lying around her lab in London and run the tests on those instead. The real question is *motive*. *Why* does Nadira Khan want everyone to believe Driftosaurus is a hoax? Is it just because a genuine megalosaurus on the island would prove her theories wrong?'

'Someone could have paid her to do it,' Scott suggested.

Emily looked up, chewing her pen. 'Like who?'

'What about that Raven company? If they really wanted to build a theme park on the quarry site, a significant dinosaur find would be a disaster. It'd hold up their plans for ages while the scientists go in and do a full study. That's a motive to try to make the fossil look like a fake.'

Emily frowned. 'It's a good idea. But there's no evidence that Raven Resorts have bought that land. And even if they had, why would Professor Khan get involved in anything so dodgy, even for money?'

Jack grinned. 'You're right, Em. Scott's talking rubbish. Khan obviously just hates Professor Atherton for some reason and she's pretending the fossil is a hoax to make him look stupid! Don't forget, it was her idea to invite the press along and make a big deal of it.'

Scott rolled his eyes. 'And which pre-schooler did you nick that highly-sophisticated theory from?'

Emily slammed her notebook shut. 'Come on! It's time we found out a little more about Professor Nadira Khan. To the library!'

—

Only one of the computers in the tiny Castle Key library was free. The friends huddled round the screen as Scott typed NADIRA KHAN into the search box and scrolled through pages of results. Khan had written hundreds of articles on palaeontology, as well as three books, but the most interesting part was that Atherton and Khan had been writing papers attacking each other's research for decades. Atherton's 1992 paper, *Coprolite Discovery Proves Megalosaurus on Castle Key Island* was followed the next year by Khan's article, *Coprolite Data Seriously Flawed: A Reply to Atherton*. Then Atherton was right back at her with *Why Khan's Arguments Miss the Point*. And so it went on.

'Wow,' Emily whistled. 'I never knew science was so brutal. Looks like Jack's theory is right. These two can't stand each other!'

Scott leaned back and raked his hands through his hair. 'I'm still not buying it. Khan has been attacking Atherton in these journals for years. But faking test results is a whole different ball game. Her reputation as a scientist would be on the line if anyone found out.'

Typical, Jack thought. *Why can't Scott ever admit he's wrong and I'm right?* And now the two girls working on a school project at the next computer were batting their eyelashes at Scott, and Scott was pretending he hadn't noticed – but he clearly *had* because he was flipping his floppy fringe in that way he thought made him look cool. Jack couldn't bear any more of this! He got up and began to mooch among the bookshelves. He found himself in a section called *King Arthur and Related Legends.* He skimmed the book titles: *Perceval, the Story of the Grail; Lancelot, the Knight of the Cart; Tristan and Iseult . . .* Wasn't Tristan the name of that knight Izzy and Skye were going on about?

Jack pulled the book from the shelf and started to flick through it. Ten minutes later he was sitting on the floor still reading. This stuff was *awesome*! It was so jam-packed with murder, betrayal and people snogging people they shouldn't be snogging, it made *EastEnders* look like *Sesame Street.*

'Come and look at this!'

Jack suddenly realized that Emily and Scott were calling him. He slid the book back on the shelf, and peered over Scott's shoulder. The article on the screen had been scanned in from a student newspaper, dated January 1979:

London University graduate student, Nadira Khan, today issued an official apology concerning a paper she recently published in the *British Journal of Paleontology*. Khan (22) claimed to have identified a new species of velociraptor, but it was later revealed to be a case of mistaken identity, due to a laboratory mix-up. 'I foolishly relied on tests that had been conducted by another member of the research team,' Miss Khan told our reporter. It is believed that the mistake was made by Harold Atherton (27) . . .

'And Jack Carter gets it right again!' Jack crowed. He patted Scott on the back. 'I told you Nadira Khan hated Atherton. Now we have proof. It was his fault she published a paper with a mistake in it which made her look like an idiot. She's been waiting thirty years to get her own back!'

Scott scowled and pretended to be concentrating on the screen, but Emily nodded slowly. 'Of course! Remember Margaret said something about how rushing into things had got Atherton into trouble before? This must be what she was talking about.' She took out her notebook and spoke the words as she wrote. 'Nadira Khan, classic motive – revenge!'

Jack smirked at Scott. 'Yeah, *revenge*. The old favourite. Like when King Mark of Cornwall wanted to murder Tristan because he'd been getting a bit up close and personal with his wife, Iseult.'

Scott gaped at his brother as if he'd started speaking in Ancient Greek. How did Jack know this stuff? Had he started listening at school for the first time in his life? Or was he making it up? It was annoying enough that Jack was right about Professor Khan having it in for Atherton, without him suddenly being able to spout medieval literature as if he knew what he was talking about!

—

Case closed! Emily thought, as she walked back to The Lighthouse to help her mum with some cleaning jobs. She could hardly wait to write up her notes so they could hand the entire case to D. I. Hassan at Carrickstowe Police Station. Wrapping up an investigation in a single afternoon had to be her personal best, so why wasn't she feeling more pleased with herself? 'You're right, Drift,' she said to the little dog trotting along at her side. 'It was almost *too* easy!' Operation Dinosaur had not exactly tested her investigative skills and powers of deduction.

But when Emily opened the front door of The Lighthouse, she realized that maybe the case wasn't quite closed after all. Mum was sitting behind the antique table she used as a reception desk, checking in a new guest. There was nothing unusual about that. Mum was talking at a hundred miles an hour.

There was nothing unusual about that either. What *was* unusual was the new guest herself – a woman with an upright posture, a camel-coloured coat and a scarf over her hair.

Nadira Khan was back in town.

Eleven

Danger on the Moor

H er heart in her mouth, Emily shot back out of the door.

She leaned against the wall to think. Why had Nadira Khan returned to Castle Key? Was she here simply to gloat over Atherton's misfortune? Or did she have plans to wreak further revenge on her old enemy? Emily imagined Khan breaking into Coastguard Cottage and . . . and *what*? Wrecking the laboratory? Kidnapping

Margaret? One thing Emily knew for sure: she was going to have to keep Nadira Khan under twenty-four-hour surveillance.

She called Scott's number on her mobile. Scott immediately figured out *exactly* why Khan was back. 'It's obvious!' he said. 'If Khan faked those results in her lab to make it look as if the dinosaur is a hoax, she needs to sabotage the tests that Atherton is running himself. Otherwise his results might eventually show the fossil is a genuine megalosaurus. She can't take the risk that people will believe his word over hers and uncover her deception.'

'Of course!' Emily murmured, marvelling at Scott's super-logical brain. She crept to a window and peeped into the guest lounge. *Red alert!* Nadira Khan was already on the move! She'd left her overnight bag behind the desk with Mum and was heading for the door. Emily shrank back against the wall. 'OK, here's the plan,' she whispered into the phone. 'If we move fast we can catch her red-handed . . .'

Scott and Jack threw on their coats and barrelled out of Stone Cottage. They cut through the churchyard, took the footpath to the coast road and headed west, sprinting as fast as they could on the slippery veneer of frozen snow. They had to get to Coastguard Cottage to stop Nadira Khan before she could sabotage Atherton's tests. Emily would catch them up as soon as she could – after phoning Margaret Atherton to warn her that trouble was on its way.

The boys ran on, their lungs burning in the cold air. At any moment, they expected to hear Professor Khan's Mini behind them, and to have to leap off the road to hide as she passed. But to Scott's surprise, the first sound he heard over the rasping of his own breath was not a car, but his phone ringing.

Emily's voice was urgent. 'You're not going to believe this! Khan *isn't* heading for the Athertons' house. I tracked her Mini through the binoculars. She's taken the main road across South Moor. I've lost sight of her now, but there's only one place she can be heading.'

'The quarry!' Scott panted.

'Meet me by the twisted trees on the cart track,' Emily instructed. 'We've got to find out what she's up to!'

By the time they reached the quarry the friends were exhausted by their high-speed trek across the moor. A solitary car was parked near the gates, the blue metal bright against the black and white landscape of snow, sky and rock. A single set of footprints led up the hill and through the broken fence towards the mound where Driftosaurus lay hidden.

Emily, Scott, Jack and Drift crept as far up the slope as they dared, and crouched behind a gorse bush, its spindly branches heavily clotted with snow. Emily peeked out. On the other side of the fence a lonely figure was silhouetted against a sky the soft grey of pigeon feathers. Nadira Khan pulled back the tarpaulin cover. It flapped in a gust of wind, the noise ringing out like a gunshot in the silence.

'What's she doing to Driftosaurus?' Jack whispered.

'Just staring at it,' Scott hissed. 'Now she's taking photos.'

Emily shifted position. Drift kept butting his head against her knees, whimpering softly. She gave him a reassuring pat. Strange, she thought, Drift didn't usually make a fuss during a Stake Out.

Khan straightened up, rubbing her arms against the cold. Then she half jogged, half slid down the slope, clutching her headscarf to stop the wind snatching it from her hair.

Moments later, Emily heard the engine start and the Mini pull away. She looked down the hill to watch it go, but it had disappeared. To her dismay, she realized the fence and the track had disappeared too. In fact, she could barely see the gorse bush right in front of her!

Everything was veiled in dense white mist.

Emily couldn't believe it. She'd been so intent on tailing Khan's every move she'd completely missed the signs: the swollen grey clouds, the strengthening wind. And now snow was falling thick and fast. Drift had tried to warn her but she hadn't listened. It was a full-blown blizzard! And they'd walked right into it!

No need for alarm, Emily told herself. *Assess the situation and react in a calm and rational manner.* That's what it always said in *Survival Tips for Secret Agents.* She ran through a quick situation report in her head. The quarry was fenced off but there were many other hazards on the moors: streams and bogs and treacherous gullies. The biggest danger, however, was getting lost. Even though Emily knew the terrain well, the familiar landmarks had disappeared. It would soon be dark and the temperature was dropping fast. They had to get off the moor quickly or hypothermia would be a serious risk.

The first priority was to let someone know where they were. Emily took out her phone to call home, but there was no signal.

'I haven't got a signal either,' Scott said, shaking his phone in irritation. 'And no GPS signal.'

'Brr! Come on!' Jack urged. 'Let's get out of here.' He began to stride down the hill. Within three steps he'd been swallowed up by the fog.

'First rule!' Emily snapped as she pulled him back. 'We stay together at all times.' She took her compass from her bag and checked her bearings. 'We won't go cross-country to the cart track. We'll head west till we meet the quarry road, and follow it back to the main road. There's less chance of getting lost.'

Scott nodded grimly. He zipped his jacket up over his chin and pulled down his woollen cap. He never thought he'd be envious of Jack's teddy bear hat, but he was now! Gritting his teeth he marched through the knee-deep snow. The wind drove snowflakes into his face, stinging his cheeks like icy needles.

Jack began chanting like a US marine. 'I don't know but I've been told, your nose can drop off in the cold . . .'

'*Really* not helping!' Scott growled. He tried to harness the power of positive thinking: *hot chocolate, hot bath, hot chocolate, hot bath* . . . He repeated the words with every weary step. He was so cold even his bones were hurting. Just when he thought he couldn't lift his foot one more time, Drift barked.

Emily stopped. Jack walked into her. Scott walked into Jack.

'Look!' Emily cried. 'Professor Khan's car!'

'She must have seen us and stopped to give us a lift,' Jack laughed. 'Awesome!'

Scott stumbled towards the Mini. Who cared that Khan was their prime suspect? The car would be warm and dry! He reached for the handle of the passenger door, the sodden wool of his glove sticking to the frozen metal.

Nothing happened.

'Why won't Khan unlock the doors?' Jack yelled over the wailing wind.

Emily looked up from peering in through the windows. 'Because,' she said, 'she's not in the car!'

That's when Scott noticed that the Mini was wedged deep into a snowdrift. 'She must have skidded off the road and got stuck.'

'Oh, no!' Emily gasped from the other side of the car. 'This is not good!' The fear in her voice was unmistakable. Scott and Jack ran to her side and found her staring down at a trail of footprints. Drift, almost up to his nose in snow, was looking up at her, his ears bedraggled and drooping.

'Looks like Khan decided to walk back to the main road,' Scott said.

Jack stamped impatiently. 'Let's get going then. We'll probably catch her up.'

Emily sighed. 'Yeah, we probably would, *if she was actually going in the right direction.*'

Scott and Jack stared at her. Emily showed them the compass. 'The main road is south of here. Nadira Khan is walking due north. She's heading right back onto the moor.'

'What a dingbat!' Jack snorted. 'I thought professors were meant to be brainy. Never mind. As soon as we get back to civilization we'll call the Mountain Rescue people to go and find her.'

Emily clutched his arm. 'That could be too late. What if she's fallen into a gully? If she's lying injured in this weather she could be dead within an hour!'

Jack felt his heart drop right down into his snow-sodden boots. Somehow he knew what was coming next. 'You mean . . .'

Emily nodded. 'We have to go and find her.'

Scott closed his eyes and when he spoke his voice sounded as if it were coming from the bottom of a deep well. 'Em's right. We can't just leave her out here.'

Emily picked Drift up and held him in her arms. And then the friends did something they'd never done before: they joined in a group hug, arms locked, foreheads pressed together, as if to gather strength from each other for the mission that lay ahead.

And at that moment a blood-curdling howl pierced the mist.

Twelve

The Blizzard Mission

'*Wolves!*' Jack gasped.

Terror slid its icy tentacles down his spine. *Wolves have hunted down Professor Khan. And now that they have a taste for human flesh, they'll be hungry for more . . .*

'There are no wolves on Castle Key!' Emily said firmly. 'It was just a dog.'

'Sounds carry a long way in these conditions,'

Scott said knowledgeably.

'How come you're an expert on blizzard sound effects all of a sudden, Scott of the Antarctic?' Jack snapped. He was fed up – not to mention freezing and famished – and now they had to go tramping off over the stupid moor again. This was like one of those expeditions to the South Pole in the olden days when everything went wrong and they all had to eat their boots. He'd never thought he could actually come to *hate* snow! Suddenly he brightened up. He'd bought three bars of chocolate from Dotty's at lunchtime. He waged war with his conscience. Did he really *have* to share them? But his conscience won the battle. He fished the precious bars out of his coat pocket, where they were tangled up with a length of wire he'd picked up from the broken fence at the quarry, and held them out.

'Jack, you're a star!' Emily exclaimed. 'We'll share one now and keep the rest for later.' She fished in her coat pocket and found a treat for Drift too. 'Now, let's get going.'

Heads down, they set off into the vast white wilderness again, following the trail of footprints and stopping every few minutes to call Professor Khan's name.

Before long Jack was dizzy with exhaustion. His wet jeans clung to his legs like seaweed. He longed to curl up in the snow and go to sleep. 'It feels like we're walking in circles!' he grumbled.

'We are!' Emily had been keeping a close eye on

the compass. 'Professor Khan is totally lost.'

After what seemed like hours of trudging through the fog, Jack stumbled and almost fell into a ravine. Scott caught him just in time. 'We have to turn back!' Scott called to Emily. 'I don't think Jack can go much further.'

Jack was about to protest. How dare Scott call him a weakling! But, in fact, his brother was right. He really *couldn't* keep going. But suddenly Drift pricked up his ears into Listening Formation. Jack held his breath and at last he heard the feeble cry. 'I'm down here! Help!'

Drift raced off down the steep bank. When the friends caught up, they found Professor Khan lying near a landslide of rocks. Her brown skin had taken on a blue-grey tinge and her eyes fluttered under closed lids. Drift had curled up next to her to warm her.

Emily dropped to her knees and unpacked the first aid kit from her bag. She pulled the foil survival blanket from its little pouch and wrapped it round Professor Khan's shoulders. 'Scott, water! Jack, chocolate!' she commanded, holding out her hand like a surgeon waiting for the nurse to pass a scalpel.

After a few sips from Emily's water bottle and a piece of chocolate, Professor Khan revived a little. 'I slipped on the rocks,' she said, wincing in pain as Scott helped her to sit up. 'I've twisted my ankle. It was stupid to set out on my own, I know. I wasn't thinking straight. I hit my head on the steering wheel when I went off the road.'

'You're probably concussed,' Scott told her as Emily

unwrapped a bandage. 'We'll help you back and you can keep warm in the car while we dig it out of the snowdrift.'

Emily finished binding Professor Khan's ankle. 'Right, let's get going!'

Jack groaned. 'Can't we rest here for a bit?'

Emily was ready to drop too, but she knew they had to muster their last scraps of energy and get back to the car. There was little chance they'd survive the night out in the open. 'It's not far,' she said briskly, tapping the compass. 'I've plotted the direct route back.' And with that she picked up her satchel and Professor Khan's small brown briefcase and waited, hands on hips, with Drift at her side.

Scott helped Professor Khan up and she hobbled along with her arm round his shoulders. Jack trailed along behind them. The only thing that kept him going was rage! 'Bossy boots!' he muttered under his breath at Emily's back. *It's not far? Yeah, right!* And of course, Scott had taken her side. *Typical!* But to his amazement, Emily *was* right. Suddenly the blue Mini was looming up out of the mist. Jack punched the air in triumph. He couldn't wait to turn the heater up to max and bask in the warmth.

But when Professor Khan began to fumble for her car keys – first in one coat pocket, then the other – he knew that disaster was about to strike. It was just the kind of day he was having.

'Oh, no,' Khan gulped. 'The keys must have slipped out of my pocket when I fell.'

Despair washed over them all. On top of the fog, the snow and the cold, the light was now fading fast. No one had the strength to walk back and search in the snow for the keys.

It was Scott who spoke first. 'We have to break into the car. Have you got a wire coat-hanger, Em?'

'Do I *look* like I carry coat hangers around with me?' Emily's temper had finally stretched to breaking point. 'What for? Hanging up a dress in an emergency?'

Scott glared at her. 'No need to bite my head off! I just need something to slide down inside the door.'

Jack couldn't bear it. He stuffed his hands in his pockets and turned to march off into the darkness. He had no idea where he was going, but anywhere had to be better than this. Suddenly he felt something in his pocket that made him turn back. 'Would this do?' he asked.

Scott stared at the knot of wire dangling from Jack's soggy glove. He nodded and without a word, took the wire, straightened it out and shaped the end into a hook. Then he fed it down between the window and the frame on the passenger door and jiggled it about a bit. He wasn't really sure what he was doing, but suddenly he felt the wire catch on something. He pulled it up. Nothing! He pushed it down again. He heard a click.

He tried the handle and to his astonishment the door opened.

'Ta da!' he crowed, pulling the door open and bowing like a chauffeur.

Emily hugged him.

Jack grinned and murmured 'Skill!'

Between them they settled Professor Khan on the back seat with her ankle propped up. Emily hot-wired the ignition – a trick she'd perfected during Operation Skeleton – so that they could run the heater. Emily sat in the driver's seat with Drift on her lap. Scott bagged the passenger seat and Jack had to squash between them in the middle, but he was so happy to be thawing out in the warmth he didn't even object.

'That's better!' he sighed, sharing out a packet of stale cheese sandwiches he found in the glove compartment. 'So, Scotto? Is there something you want to share with us? My Secret Life as a Joyrider?'

'He's been sneakily reading my *Survival Tips for Secret Agents*,' Emily laughed.

Scott shook his head. 'If you keep your ears open at school it's amazing what you learn. The Bateman twins are always bragging about the cars they've nicked!'

'We're lucky I've hung on to this old banger for so long,' Professor Khan laughed from the back. 'Modern cars have all kinds of security systems to stop people breaking in.'

'So, how did you do it?' Emily asked.

In truth, Scott wasn't really sure *how* he'd done it. He'd just jiggled the wire and hoped for the best! But he wasn't going to let Emily know that. He tapped his nose mysteriously. 'If I told you that I'd have to kill you!'

Emily laughed. Then she yawned and shook her head. 'Come on,' she said. 'The sooner we start digging the car out, the sooner we can get home.'

'Did anyone ever tell you you're a *bully*, Em?' Jack complained. But he climbed out and helped scoop snow away from around the car using the sandwich box and some tiny shovels from Professor Khan's palaeontology kit in the boot. Drift dug valiantly with his paws.

When they thought they'd cleared enough snow, Scott put the car into reverse and jammed his foot on the accelerator. The wheels spun uselessly. Emily tried. Then Jack had a go. But to no avail. They dug some more. They tried spreading coats under the back wheels to give the tyres more grip. Nothing worked! At last, they admitted defeat. The Mini was well and truly stuck.

'We'll have to wait it out in the car until morning,' Scott said. 'We'll put the hazard lights on and hope someone sees us.'

'Yeah, like all the crowds cruising past for an evening out at the abandoned quarry in the middle of a snowstorm,' Jack scoffed.

Jack tried to make himself comfortable. Emily's elbow was digging into his ribs. Scott was playing games on his phone which was making annoying beeping noises. Professor Khan had fallen asleep in the back and was snoring loudly. The car, which had seemed such a haven of cosiness, now felt cramped and stuffy – even with the windows open a crack so they wouldn't suffocate. There was no way Jack could stand a whole night of this! Suddenly he had an awesome idea. 'Let's build a snow cave! I saw Bear Grylls make one on TV.'

Scott wasn't persuaded. 'Yeah, well, Bear Grylls didn't have a perfectly good car to shelter in, did he?'

'We should conserve our energy,' Emily said.

'But we've already dug a big hole in the snowdrift next to the car,' Jack coaxed. 'We just need to hollow it out a bit more. And,' he added craftily, 'then you could make a fire.' He knew how much Emily loved lighting fires with her fire-steel and tinderbox.

'OK,' Emily agreed. 'It'll keep us busy at least.' She and Drift set to work again alongside Jack and, a few moments later, Scott climbed out of the car and reluctantly joined the work party. It was completely dark now and still snowing hard.

All of a sudden Drift stopped digging. He stared into the night, his hackles raised and his ears quivering like arrows.

'Listen!' Jack breathed. 'I can hear those wolves again.'

'There are no wolves on Castle Key!' Scott and Emily chorused.

But then they heard it too.

And this time the howling was much, much closer.

Thirteen

Wolf Attack

Emily *knew* there were no wolves on Castle Key.

At least her *head* knew there were no wolves on Castle Key. Her heart wasn't so sure. It was too busy trying to break out of her ribcage and run away.

The howling was growing louder and louder.

And now Emily could hear the pounding of animal paws and the steam-engine rattle of animal panting.

'Don't be scared,' she murmured to Drift, trying to keep the terror out of her voice.

'Quick!' Scott hissed, pulling her by the arm. 'Everyone back in the car!'

Emily turned to scoop Drift up. But he'd gone. '*DR-I-I-I-FT!*' she screamed, wrenching away from Scott's grip. She caught sight of the tip of a black-and-tan tail disappearing into the darkness, but Scott and Jack were now both dragging her back towards the car. She struggled free again but stumbled and fell headfirst into the snow. Suddenly she felt herself swallowed up in a writhing mass of black fur and slavering jaws. She threw her hands up to protect her face. She could hear the boys' petrified shouts as they tried to pull the beasts off her.

'They're eating Emily!' Jack screamed.

But gradually Emily realized that she *wasn't* being torn limb from limb, after all. Only severely trampled on. This felt like one of Drift's ambushes when she came home from school and he'd not seen her all day – multiplied by about three million. She opened one eye and saw a familiar white ear with black spots among the tornado of black fur. 'Drift!' she gasped. She peeped through her fingers and Drift licked her nose. 'Eugggh!' Emily groaned as a second, much bigger pink tongue slobbered on her. And then a third.

'It's Tyson and Rambo!' Scott shouted, his voice

wobbling with relief. 'They think you're playing a game!' He pulled Emily to her feet and they all laughed as the two enormous Dobermans rolled around in the snow with Drift.

'Maybe they got lost in the blizzard too,' Jack said.

As he watched the dogs play, Scott noticed smudges of blood blossoming pink on the snow. For a moment he thought Emily had been bitten, but then he noticed that one of the dogs was limping. With Jack and Emily's help, he persuaded the big dog – it was Tyson, according to the tag on his collar – to lie down. It didn't take long to spot the problem: a thin loop of wire circled one of his back legs, just above the paw, and had pulled so tight it was biting into the flesh.

'Ouch!' Scott murmured.

Emily handed Scott the first aid kit. 'Looks like he caught it in a rabbit snare. That's what all the howling must've been about.'

'I knew it wasn't wolves really,' Jack said. He held Tyson's huge head on his lap while Scott gently eased the scissors under the wire and snipped it off. Emily dabbed antiseptic cream onto the wound.

At last, the friends huddled in the shelter of the snow cave. Emily took out her little fire-starting kit: a fire-steel to create a spark, some wood shavings steeped in resin to serve as tinder, and a little metal box to keep the fire off the wet ground. Starting the fire would be *easy* – but how were they going to keep it going without any fuel? Any grass or sticks under the snow would be soaking wet.

'You can use these if you like.' Professor Khan had woken up and was now leaning out of the car door, holding up a big box file. 'It's stuffed full of papers and notes,' she explained. 'But it's all backed up on the computer. They won't burn for long but it'll be better than nothing.'

Emily put a spark to the tinder and the boys crumpled the pages and fed them into the fire one at a time. The crackling, orange flames cheered everyone up. The three dogs curled up together close by and were soon snoring contentedly.

'Are you feeling any better now?' Emily asked Professor Khan.

'Much. The pain in my ankle is easing off. I'm sorry, I haven't thanked you properly for rescuing me.' Nadira Khan paused and frowned. 'But what were you guys doing out in a blizzard anyway?'

Scott looked at Emily and Jack. It was so long since they'd started following Professor Khan he'd almost forgotten why they were there, too. But there seemed no point in trying to conceal the truth now. 'We know you faked the test results,' he said bluntly.

Khan blinked slowly. 'What are you talking about?'

'You wanted to make it look as if our dinosaur is a hoax,' Emily said.

Khan shook her head as if trying to jiggle pieces of a puzzle into place. 'But why would I do that?'

'For *revenge*!' Jack prompted. 'Because Professor Atherton made you look stupid when he mixed up those results and you had to apologize for publishing a paper about them.'

'But I'm sure Professor Atherton didn't *mean* to get you into trouble,' Emily chipped in. 'I know he can be a bit over-enthusiastic and rush into things . . .'

'But that's not a crime, is it?' Jack asked.

'Good thing!' Scott muttered. 'Otherwise Jack'd be serving a life sentence.'

'But you're talking about something that happened over thirty years ago!' Professor Khan laughed in disbelief. 'That's all ancient history now.'

'You mean you *don't* hate him?' Jack asked. 'But what about all those papers in the journals, rubbishing each other's work?'

Professor Khan smiled. 'Yes, we have different theories and we argue about the evidence, but that's how science works! You didn't *really* think I'd faked a test result did you?'

'Er, well, yeah, we sort of thought . . . possibly . . .' Scott concentrated on feeding a paper about pterodactyls into the fire. Maybe they'd been too hasty in judging Professor Khan guilty.

But Emily wasn't giving up on her prime suspect *that* easily. 'So why did you come back to Castle Key?

And what were you doing to our dinosaur? We saw you there this afternoon.'

Professor Khan rubbed her ankle. 'Look, I admit I was furious with Harry Atherton for rushing to go public. I was convinced he was wrong about the fossil being a new species of megalosaurus, and that a silly story would end up all over the media – they'd make it sound like the next Loch Ness Monster or something! That's why I suggested the press conference – so I could make it clear that this almost certainly *wasn't* a new species. But now I'm not so sure. The results of my tests were mystifying. Odd contaminants started showing up in the sample – cleaning products and glue and all sorts. I came back to have another look to see if I could make sense of it.'

'How do we know you're telling the truth?' Emily asked.

'You'd make a good scientist, Emily! Never believe anything unless you've seen the evidence. It's all written up in my notes. You can check if you like . . .' Khan paused, looking down at the flames. 'At least you could, if you hadn't just burned them all!'

Emily stared in dismay at the charred ashes in the fire. She'd just destroyed the evidence in her own case!

Khan smiled. 'Don't worry. It's all on my laptop. I'll make copies for you in the morning.'

But Emily was leaving nothing to chance. She demanded that Professor Khan take her laptop out of her briefcase and let her read all the notes before she eventually admitted that Khan was officially *off* the list of suspects.

But that didn't change the fact that *someone* was trying to make the dinosaur look like a hoax. And if it wasn't Professor Khan, then *who was it*? 'Could anyone have tampered with the samples before you ran the tests?' Emily asked.

Nadira Khan thought for a moment. 'It's theoretically possible, I suppose . . .'

But at that moment they heard a car on the road and all thoughts of *theoretical* possibilities were chased out of their minds by the very *real* possibility of being rescued.

Fourteen

A New Suspect

J ack, Scott and Emily tumbled through the deep snow to the road, waving torches. Moments later, Margaret Atherton's Land Rover was crunching to a halt.

There was a flurry of activity as Margaret bundled everyone – including Rambo and Tyson – into the jeep, wrapped them in blankets and handed round flasks of tea. As she worked, Margaret explained that she'd started to worry when no one showed up at Coastguard

Cottage after Emily had phoned to say that they were on their way. When the blizzard set in she decided to go out and search.

'Thank goodness you did,' Nadira Khan replied. 'I'm afraid this has all been my fault. These three saved my life.'

'Four,' Emily pointed out. 'Drift found you!'

Drift looked very pleased with himself as he snuggled on Emily's lap.

'Drift's like those mountain rescue dogs,' Scott said. 'He just needs a little barrel of brandy round his neck.'

As they lurched back down the road, Jack's head nodded against Tyson's sleek shoulder. Within seconds he was fast asleep.

—

The following day the boys slept until midday – a first for Jack, although Scott was a grand master of the long lie-in. Then they spent the afternoon in dressing gowns in front of the fire. Aunt Kate had been furious with them at first for wandering around on the moor in a snowstorm. But she'd soon softened when she learned that they had rescued Professor Khan. She'd plied them with hot baths, hot chocolate and hot water bottles and even agreed that Tyson and Rambo could stay at Stone Cottage for the time being, and arranged for the vet to come and check Tyson's injured leg.

Now the dogs were snoozing on the hearth rug. Jack was using Tyson as a pillow, a plate of Aunt Kate's cherry cake balanced on his stomach, watching an old Agent Diamond film on TV.

Scott sprawled on the sofa, surfing the web on his phone. Suddenly he sat up. 'Look at this!' he shouted, kicking Jack's arm in his excitement.

'Ouch! You made me drop my cake!' Jack grumbled. 'What is it? Some new dancing cat video?' He fed the cake crumbs to Tyson and Rambo.

'Think about it. If Professor Khan didn't fake the tests on Driftosaurus, who else had access to those samples?' Scott demanded.

'Dunno,' Jack murmured. He was far too warm and comfortable to think. Scott could phone Emily at The Lighthouse if he wanted to play Twenty Questions.

'Her research assistant, of course,' Scott said impatiently. 'Melvin Spencer! He really didn't like the idea of the dinosaur being genuine, did he?'

'No, but old Raspberry Features didn't like the idea of *anything* much,' Jack laughed. 'He was a world class whinger. And why would *he* want to make our dinosaur look like a hoax?'

'That's what I wondered,' Scott said, 'so I've been looking him up on the internet. It turns out Melvin Spencer writes a blog called The Dino-Digger. It's meant to be all about palaeontology, but it's mostly complaints about other researchers . . .'

Jack laughed. 'The Raspberry? *Complaining?* Why am I not surprised?' He clambered walrus-like onto the sofa to look at Scott's phone. What he saw made him spit cake crumbs across the carpet; they were instantly hoovered up by Tyson and Rambo, who were starting to think they'd died and gone to dog heaven. Beneath a photo of Melvin Spencer's smirking face was the headline: CASTLE KEY FRAUD: BIGGEST HOAX SINCE LOCH NESS MONSTER!

'How dare he!' Jack spluttered. 'The Loch Ness monster is real! I saw it with my own eyes when we were on holiday in Scotland.'

Scott rolled his eyes. 'That was a large *seal*! Anyway, we're not starting that argument again. Look at the date on this blog post.'

Jack glanced at the date, still brooding over the Loch Ness incident. Why did no one ever believe him? 'What about it?'

'It was posted the morning after we discovered Driftosaurus.'

'So?'

'That was *before* Professor Khan and Melvin Spencer came to Castle Key. The Raspberry hadn't even *seen* the fossil yet,' Scott spelled out.

Jack finally saw what Scott was getting at. 'But he was *already* mouthing off on his blog that the dinosaur was a hoax?'

'Exactly. And then look at his *next* blog post from a

few days later. This one is after he and Khan had taken the samples to London.'

Jack began to read. The sneering tone made his toes curl.

> . . . tests confirm that the so-called giant megalosaurus reported by Cornish 'nutty professor' Harry Atherton is a hoax – and a feeble one at that. Reality Check! These bones are no older than ten thousand years. And I personally identified traces of at least six (yes, six!) modern substances in the samples, including glue, detergent and hair gel! Look out for a woolly mammoth with excellent personal hygiene and a glue-sniffing habit . . .

Scott took a piece of Jack's cherry cake and explained his theory as he munched. 'The first entry saying the dinosaur was a hoax was picked up by loads of other bloggers and Twitter feeds. It went viral. The Raspberry suddenly realized he was going to look a total dork if the dinosaur turned out to be genuine, so he decided not to take any chances. He made *certain* it was proved to be a hoax by replacing the real sample with some random old bone he found – adding a few dollops of soap and glue and stuff for good measure.'

'Yep! That sounds about right.' Jack stretched back out on the hearth rug with the dogs. 'I can't wait to tell Em we've solved Operation Dinosaur.'

'*We?*' Scott snorted, throwing a cushion at his brother. 'Er, remind me exactly which part *you* came up with?'

—

Emily's parents insisted she spend the day at home resting too, so it was the next morning when she and Drift called at Stone Cottage. Emily was hugely impressed with Scott's detective work. 'Of course,' she agreed. 'And remember when we were escaping from the Brussels sprout soup, we heard The Raspberry crashing about near the boxes of samples in the hall. He was probably already tampering with the evidence then!' Under the heading *Prime Suspect* in her notebook, Emily crossed out *Nadira Khan* and wrote in *Melvin Spencer*. 'We have to go and warn Professor Atherton,' she said. 'We can tell Professor Khan at the same time. I heard Mum order a taxi to Coastguard Cottage for her first thing this morning.'

But before setting off, there was one other job to do – arranging the return of Tyson and Rambo to their owner. Scott and Jack had secretly been putting it off because they loved having the dogs around. But Emily had tracked down the details for Trimble & Sons, the company that owned the quarry, and she dialled their number.

To her surprise, the secretary who answered had no record of a security guard working at the Castle Key site.

'That can't be right,' Emily insisted. 'We've seen him there! We have his dogs, Rambo and Tyson.'

The secretary's tone became frosty. 'Haven't you kids got anything better to do than make prank phone calls?'

What planet did that secretary live on, Jack wondered, if she thought kids went round phoning up quarry companies claiming to have rescued imaginary dogs belonging to imaginary security guards just for kicks?

'The dogs will have to come with us for now,' Scott said. 'We'll search for the mystery security guard after we've been to Coastguard Cottage.'

—

The sun shone down from a clear blue sky on the small procession of three friends and three dogs. Melting snow dripped from every branch. Rambo and Tyson trotted along behind Drift, eagerly awaiting his every command. Drift was more than happy to have two new recruits to the canine division of the investigations team. There'd been several occasions during previous cases when a pair of ferocious-looking Doberman bodyguards would have come in very useful. He'd soon have them trained up as his personal SWAT team.

They were halfway up the coast road when a red van pulled up behind them. Russ Kerrow wound down the window. 'You going to the Atherton place? Hop in if you want a lift,' he called. 'We're on our way up there to finish cleaning the observatory now the snow's gone.'

The friends squeezed into the back of the van.

'You kids got yourselves some new pets there?' Russ chuckled – without dislodging the cigarette that hung from his mouth.

'Anyone want to come in the front with me?' Liam shouted over the rock beat on his headphones. 'It must be a squash back there with Rambo and Tyson.'

'Emily wants to!' Jack called back cheekily. He'd noticed that Emily had a bit of a crush on Liam Kerrow, and couldn't resist stirring.

'Do not!' Emily snapped. 'Thank you very much,' she added, remembering her manners. She spent the rest of the short journey in uncomfortable silence, while Scott explained why they had the Dobermans with them. It wasn't *only* that she was flustered by Jack's stupid teasing; she was also plagued by the maddening feeling that someone had said something that would crack the investigation wide open.

But, try as she might, she just couldn't put her finger on what it was.

Fifteen

Criminal Damage

Margaret led the friends through to the kitchen where Professor Khan was sitting talking to Professor Atherton, her bandaged ankle resting on a basketwork footstool. Scott quickly explained his suspicions about Melvin Spencer.

Nadira Khan frowned. 'I had no idea he was posting such nonsense on his blog. Melvin has only been working with me for a few months. He's a very smart young man, but this is most unprofessional behaviour. As soon as I get back to London I'll carry out a full investigation. Meanwhile, if it's OK with you,' she turned to Harry Atherton, 'I'd like to stay on here for a while. We could run a fresh batch of tests together.'

Atherton beamed at her. 'I'd be honoured, Nadira. It's been far too long since we've worked side by side. Margaret can take us to the quarry to collect new samples this afternoon.'

Margaret didn't exactly look thrilled at the idea. 'What if I already had plans?'

'Counting your baskets, you mean?' Atherton laughed.

Margaret sighed. But eventually she gave into her brother, as she always did.

At last, Scott thought, *with the two rival professors joining forces, and no interference from weasels like Melvin Spencer, we'll soon know the truth.*

After several slices of Margaret's Christmas cake, the friends set off for the quarry to hunt for the mystery security guard. *I hope we don't find him,* Jack thought as they squelched along tracks boggy with the melting snow. *Then we could keep Tyson and Rambo forever!* He hadn't quite thought through how Dad was going to take it when they got home to their flat in London with two huge Dobermans, but he'd work something out. *Perhaps the guard doesn't even exist,* Jack thought. He could be a phantom security guard, wandering the moors with his demon hounds – like something from one of Old Bob's legends.

When they reached the quarry there was only one vehicle in the car park – an old truck that Emily recognized as belonging to Graham Fothergill and his group of alien scientists, who were staying at The Lighthouse. As they approached the fence, she caught sight of Graham's tin foil hat sparkling in the sunlight as he dashed up and down the dinosaur mound waving a satellite dish in the air. Nearby, the garden gnome guy – his face almost hidden by thick goggles – gave a thumbs-up signal to Molly Dunnock, who was kneeling over Driftosaurus holding up two electrical cables with large crocodile clips on the ends.

Emily exchanged glances with Scott and Jack, but before they could investigate further, a white van roared up the road and parked next to the truck. Emily dived out of sight behind a rocky crag, pulling the boys and dogs in behind her. They all watched as the security guard climbed out and puffed his way up the slope.

'This is private land!' he shouted. 'And that's criminal damage, that is!' He pointed at the broken fence.

At that moment Molly touched her cables to Driftosaurus, as if trying to shock his fossilized heart into life. There was a flash and a bang followed by a distinct whiff of burning wire. 'Voltage way too high!' she muttered to the plump man, who began twiddling buttons on a portable electricity generator.

'People trampling around up here non-stop!' the guard ranted. 'That crowd of hippy nutters was up here again this morning; dancing around, singing about dragons. Should be locked up, all of you!'

Graham looked down at the guard from the top of the mound. 'You seem to be channelling a lot of anger,' he commented in a reasonable tone. 'Have you tried protecting your brainwaves with tin foil?'

'Think you're funny, do you? Well, we'll see who's laughing when I get the police after you!'

What for? Emily wondered. *Applying electrical currents to a dinosaur without due care and attention?* She could just imagine Detective Inspector Hassan's face if that case landed on his desk!

The guard began to stomp back down the slope. Emily reached into her bag for her binoculars to get a better look at his van but, to her horror, the bag slipped from her shoulder and fell to the ground with a thud. She held her breath, but it was no good. The guard turned towards the rocks. 'Another bunch of loonies, no doubt! Come on out, whoever you are!'

Brilliant! Emily screamed at herself. *You've only gone and given away our position during a surveillance operation!* She stepped out from behind the rocks, her face flushing crimson with shame. Scott, Jack, Drift, Tyson and Rambo all filed out behind her. For some reason Jack had his hands up, as if expecting to be shot on sight.

The guard glowered at Tyson and Rambo, almost speechless with rage. *Almost*, but not quite. 'YOU KIDS NICKED MY DOGS!' he bellowed.

The two Dobermans shrank back and cowered behind Drift.

'We didn't *steal* them,' Scott protested. 'They were lost in the blizzard. We came to give them back.'

The guard marched over and grabbed Tyson and Rambo by their collars.

'You'll need to change the dressing on Tyson's leg . . .' Jack began to explain.

But the man was already dragging the dogs away and bundling them roughly into the back of his van.

Drift's ears drooped. Emily picked him up and gave him a cuddle. Jack looked as if he needed a cuddle too as he watched the van screech off down the road, but Emily wasn't going there. She gave him a pat on the arm instead. Then she sat down on a rock and started writing in her notebook. At least they'd gathered some intelligence on the mystery guard. She jotted down the registration number of his van.

'It seems that the secretary was telling the truth,' she said. 'This guy isn't working for the quarry company. There was no Trimble & Sons logo on the side of the vehicle.'

'Yeah, the only marking on the van was a curved letter M on the door,' Scott added.

'So if he's not working for Trimble, who *is* he

working for?' Jack asked grumpily. 'And what's he doing marching around giving out orders like he owns the place?'

Emily got to her feet. 'That's what I want to know. While we're waiting for Atherton and Khan to come up with the results on the new set of fossil samples, I suggest we focus our attention on finding out more about this guy.'

Jack's attention was already firmly focused on the guard, but for a different reason. He was wondering whether he could report him to the RSPCA for mistreating Tyson and Rambo.

Sixteen

Door-to-Door Enquiries

Scott gaped at Emily over his hot chocolate. He couldn't take in what she was telling him. It was two days later and he'd been woken early by a frantic phone message from Emily at The Lighthouse, calling an emergency meeting at Dotty's café. 'I don't believe it!' he repeated.

But Emily nodded slowly. 'It's true. Professor Khan told me this morning. The new tests she's running with

125

Professor Atherton are turning out exactly the same as the ones she did in London: the fossilized bones are from some kind of prehistoric mammal – probably a woolly mammoth – and they've found traces of all those weird chemicals again.'

Jack was so flabbergasted he tipped the whole jug of maple syrup onto his pancakes. 'But how? Melvin Spencer wasn't around to get his paws on the sample this time. Unless he's secretly returned to the island disguised as a blueberry instead of a raspberry or something!'

Emily removed the syrup jug from Jack's hand and shook her head. 'Professor Khan checked. Spencer's at a conference in Paris.'

Scott sighed. *Another* prime suspect was in the clear! This investigation was turning out to be their most baffling yet. They'd spent the last two days trying to track down the elusive security guard, but the van's registration number that Emily had carefully noted down turned out to be false, and a search of companies starting with M had revealed no matches with the curved black letter on the van. The guard seemed to have disappeared into thin air – along with Rambo, Tyson and the white van. *Abducted by giant lizards from outer space*, Jack had suggested.

Scott was convinced that the guard held the key to solving the mystery of the dinosaur hoax. For a start, despite all his threats, he hadn't called the police to remove anyone from the quarry – even though there had been a constant stream of visitors, and the fence had been smashed down several times. Scott suspected that the reason the guard hadn't involved the police was because he didn't want to draw attention to his own shady activities – whatever they might be . . .

Deep in thought, Scott looked up as an elderly man entered the café, stooping under the weight of a newspaper delivery bag. He dropped a copy of *The Carrickstowe Times* on the counter, pulled up a bar stool and ordered a cappuccino, chatting with Dotty as she frothed the milk.

'Have you heard the latest on this dinosaur up on South Moor?' he asked. 'They're saying it's definitely a fake now.'

Scott didn't mean to eavesdrop but once he'd picked up the key words 'dinosaur' and 'fake', his ears couldn't help tuning in to the conversation.

The newspaper man tapped the front page of *The Carrickstowe Times*. 'Says here "an anonymous source" revealed that local residents planted the phony dinosaur skeleton in an attempt to prevent Raven Resorts building a theme park on the old quarry. You're a local resident, Dotty,' he chuckled. 'What have you been up to?'

Dotty wiped her hands on her apron. 'I'm far too busy to go lugging dinosaurs around the moors,' she laughed. 'Fake *or* genuine.'

Suddenly Scott remembered Emily telling him that her dad was organizing a group of local residents to protest against the theme park idea. Was it possible that Driftosaurus really *was* a hoax, and that Mr Wild's HOCKI group had something to do with it?

Emily saw the look in Scott's eye and somehow read his mind. 'Oh, no! No way! You really think my dad could have done something *that* major and I wouldn't know anything about it? My parents can't even keep my birthday presents secret!'

Scott could see her point. 'What about other members of HOCKI then?' he asked. 'Could someone have done it without your dad knowing?'

'It's possible, I suppose,' Emily admitted. 'But we'd need to make door-to-door enquiries to rule out everyone on the island!'

At the counter the newspaper man was draining the last of his coffee. 'Right! Better get these delivered.' He groaned as he bent to pick up his bag. 'Ooh, my back's giving me some gyp today.'

Suddenly Scott had a brilliant idea. He darted across to the counter. 'We'll deliver the rest of those papers for you if you like.'

The old man eyed Scott suspiciously. 'Why would you want to do that?' he asked.

Good question, Scott thought. 'We're just a bit, er, bored,' he mumbled.

Once he was convinced that Scott wasn't a serial

newspaper thief, the man gratefully handed over his bag and left the café.

Jack stared at Scott. 'Am I imagining things? For a moment there I thought you just volunteered us for three hours of totally pointless hard labour?' He tried lifting the bag. 'There must be a paper in here for every house on the island!'

Scott grinned. 'Exactly! It's the perfect cover story for door-to-door enquiries. As we deliver each person's paper, we can casually mention the dinosaur hoax story on the front page and get them talking.'

'Scott, you're a genius!' Emily exclaimed. 'We sound out people's opinion about the theme park rumour. If anyone's dead against it, we can follow up with more questions.'

Jack snorted with laughter. 'And then they'll put their hands up and say, "It's a fair cop, guv. I admit I ordered a fake megalosaurus skeleton on eBay and buried it near the quarry!"'

'You don't *have* to help with this investigation if you'd rather stay here and stuff your face with pancakes,' Scott snapped.

Don't tempt me! Jack thought. But in the end he didn't want to be left out, so they divided the newspapers into three piles. Scott and Jack set off on foot, each covering half of Castle Key village. Emily took Tregower hamlet on the north coast. She stacked the papers into the basket on the back of her bike and Drift perched on top.

The friends reported back at Stone Cottage at midday and flopped in front of the fire to compare notes. Most people they'd spoken to were very worried about the rumour of a huge new resort springing up on the island. But when the subject of the dinosaur hoax came up, nobody had shown even the tiniest sign of guilt.

'It must be a world record,' Jack said. 'We've eliminated the entire population of the island from our enquiries in one morning.'

'Not quite,' Scott said. 'I suppose someone could just be a very good liar. But it's unlikely. Castle Key's a small place. Surely if Driftosaurus were a hoax, *someone* would have heard something.'

'Yeah,' Jack agreed. 'Even Mrs Loveday didn't have any gossip about it. I rest my case!'

'Which takes us right back to our original theory,' Emily argued. 'The megalosaurus is genuine but *someone* is switching the samples to make it *look* like a hoax.'

'Like who?' Jack demanded. 'We've ruled out Professor Khan and Melvin Spencer.'

'*Think!*' Emily said, twisting her hands through her chestnut curls. 'Who else has been around both times the fossil samples were collected?'

Suddenly Scott had an idea. In fact, it was such a brilliant and obvious idea he couldn't believe he hadn't had it before. 'Liam and Russ Kerrow! They were cleaning the observatory dome on Saturday afternoon when Khan and Atherton brought back the second set of samples. *And* they were around that first day when we went to see Atherton. Remember? Liam came down to the lab to give Professor Atherton a message from his dad.' Scott's heart quickened with excitement. He was sure he was on to something *The Kerrows were there both times!*

Emily looked hopeful for a moment, but then she flipped back through the pages of her notebook and shook her head. 'Sorry. It's a good theory, but it doesn't work. On that first day, the Kerrows left Coastguard Cottage at the same time as we went off in the Land Rover to collect samples.'

'That's right,' Jack said. 'We saw them loading the ladders onto the van when all the reporters turned up.'

Scott thumped a cushion on the sofa, taking out his frustration on the stupid pattern of buttercups and bluebells. *Of course!* he thought. *By the time we brought those samples back to Coastguard Cottage, the Kerrows were long gone. They couldn't have made the switch!*

Jack gazed gloomily into the fire. 'That's it. We're stuck then, aren't we? There was no one else around both times. Apart from Margaret Atherton, of course …' His voice tailed off. The friends looked at each other, the silence broken only by Drift snoring contentedly on the hearth rug, the ticking of the grandfather clock in the hall and the crackling of the flames.

No, it can't be Margaret Atherton, Emily thought. *Why would Margaret want to sabotage her own brother's work?* Margaret and Harry were obviously very close – even though they were always bickering. And Margaret only wanted the best for her brother. *The best for him! That's it!* Suddenly, it all made sense. 'Of course! It *was* Margaret. Do you remember that she said they'd been planning to move to Mexico?'

'For the amazing baskets!' Jack filled in, nodding.

'Well, that too,' Emily laughed, 'but *mainly* because the climate would be much better for Professor Atherton's health. Margaret was worried she'd never persuade him to move now we'd found the megalosaurus he's been looking for all this time. She thought he would insist on staying on Castle Key island to continue his research . . .'

Scott held up his hands for a high-five. 'Yes! Margaret is trying to convince her brother the dinosaur is a fake so he'll give up the hunt and go to Mexico. She thinks she's doing it for his own good.'

Jack grimaced. 'Tough love, you mean? Like when Dad confiscated my BMX bike so I'd do more homework – just because I did a bit badly on that history test?'

'*A bit badly?*' Scott snorted. 'Miss Taylor said it was the worst essay she'd seen in her thirty-three years of teaching.'

'Well, how did I know when she said to write about

Churchill she meant some old prime minister and not the dog in the TV advert?'

While the boys quarrelled, Emily took out her notebook. Under the heading *Prime Suspect* she crossed out *Melvin Spencer* and wrote in *Margaret Atherton*. Then she remembered that they'd been wrong twice already and added a big question mark. This time she wasn't going to jump to conclusions.

But then Jack suddenly started doing a victory dance around the room. 'I've got it!' he yelled. 'It was Ivan!'

Seventeen

Ivan the Terrible

'*Ivan?*' Scott asked. 'Who's Ivan? I thought we'd just figured out it was Margaret Atherton!'

Jack was too busy with his victory dance to answer. He shimmied round the sofa, moonwalked past Aunt Kate's desk and threw in some 'stirring-the-pot'. *Oh yeah, smooth moves!*

Next thing he knew, Scott had rugby-tackled him to the floor and was threatening to throttle him if he didn't tell them who Ivan was. Drift leaped off the rug and joined in. He *loved* tag wrestling!

'You must remember Ivan,' Jack laughed. 'The woolly mammoth.'

'*Ivan the Woolly Mammoth?*' Scott scoffed. 'Would this be a personal friend of yours? Like Donald Duck and Rudolf the Red-Nosed Reindeer?'

'Hang on, Jack's right!' Emily cut in. 'Ivan's that woolly-mammoth skeleton in the tower room. Margaret told us the first time we went to Coastguard Cottage.'

Jack grinned triumphantly. 'Never mind, Scotto. Not *everyone* is gifted with such highly advanced memory functions as me!'

Scott walloped Jack with a cushion. But he had to admit his brother was right. The woolly mammoth *was* an important clue, whatever its name was. Professor Khan said the dodgy fossil sample was probably from a woolly mammoth, and there just happened to be a woolly-mammoth skeleton right under Margaret Atherton's nose. Surely that couldn't be a coincidence.

Emily agreed. She returned to her notebook and gave Margaret Atherton's name a double underline. But she left the question mark just in case. 'I think,' she said, 'we need to pay a visit to Coastguard Cottage.'

Jack was already on his way to the door.

They formulated a plan on the way. 'Two of us interview Margaret,' Emily suggested. 'We'll say we're trying to work out whether anyone could have broken into the house and switched the samples.'

Scott nodded. 'And while Margaret is occupied with that, one of us inspects Ivan to see if he's had any recent damage.'

'Bagsy I get Ivan!' Jack blurted. Conducting a post mortem on a woolly-mammoth skeleton sounded much more fun than questioning Margaret. She might start going on about baskets again, and when you factored the risk of Brussels sprout soup into the equation, there was no competition!

—

Margaret Atherton welcomed the friends inside. 'Harry and Nadira are in the lab if you want to see them,' she said. 'They're working against the clock now. We got a call from the council this morning. If Harry can't prove the fossil is a genuine dinosaur, they'll assume it's a hoax and give the quarry company permission to continue their safety work next week.'

Scott exchanged worried glances with Emily and Jack. *Next week! We'll have to work even faster, otherwise Driftosaurus could be smashed to pieces in just a few days' time!* 'Actually, it's you we wanted to talk to, Margaret,' he said politely. 'We're trying to establish whether anyone other than Melvin Spencer could have tampered with the fossil samples.'

Margaret smiled. 'In that case, why don't you come down to the kitchen? I've just made flapjacks.'

Jack was on his third piece of flapjack when he noticed Scott shooting him sideways glances. Now Emily was twitching too. What was the matter with those two? Then he remembered: he had a date with Ivan! 'Must go to the loo,' he mumbled, snagging a fourth flapjack for the journey.

Jack hurried back up the steps and across the basket hall into the tower room. He gazed up at Ivan the Terrible on his wooden stand. The bones were stained golden brown with age. On closer inspection Jack could see metal pins and dried-up smears of old glue where loose pieces had been stuck in place to reconstruct the skeleton some time in the past.

Four legs? Check! Two tusks? Check! Ivan didn't seem to have any bits missing. But you'd only need to take a tiny shard of bone to switch for the Driftosuarus sample. And the mammoth was so, well, *mammoth*! The enormous curved tusks reached almost to the ground, but the top of the skull towered metres above Jack's head.

Jack scanned the room and noticed a stepladder propped against the wall. He quickly dragged it over, scrambled up and balanced on the top step to examine Ivan's backbone. He was about to give up when something caught his eye: a rib was missing. His heart was doing wheelies as he leaned in for a better look. *Yes!* This had been done recently. The surface of the bone was a much lighter shade where it had been snapped off. Jack reached for the camera in his pocket. This was going to be killer evidence!

Then he heard a door slam and footsteps in the corridor.

He spun round to look. The stepladder slipped.

Suddenly Jack was wobbling. Then he was teetering, tumbling, grabbing at bones to break his fall, and finally landing on the floor in an untidy heap.

'Jack! What on earth are you doing?'

Jack opened one eye and saw Scott gawping down at him. Then Emily and Margaret Atherton swam into view.

'I think he must have walked into the stepladder and tripped over!' Emily said swiftly.

'Yeah, he's so clumsy!' Scott added. '*Always* walking into things.'

Jack opened his other eye and saw the upturned point of Ivan's tusk. *Great! I'm millimetres away from being impaled by a mammoth tusk and Scott and Emily are only worried that I'll give away the investigation! At least Drift cares*, he thought, as the little dog licked his face.

'Oh, I'm so sorry,' Margaret cried, helping Jack up. 'I must have left the ladder out when I was dusting the bookshelves.'

'You were meant to be *examining* the woolly mammoth, not trying to ride on it!' Scott laughed as they left Coastguard Cottage and set off back down the coast road.

Jack was too excited to take any notice of Scott's teasing. 'We were right!' he said. 'Someone has definitely hacked a chunk off Ivan. So, unless Margaret just fancied mammoth spare ribs for a winter barbecue, we've got her.'

But Scott and Emily weren't so sure. Their interview with Margaret had shed doubt on their theory. 'After they brought the second batch of Driftosaurus samples back on Saturday,' Scott told Jack, 'Margaret dropped Harry and Nadira off at home and went straight out to Carrickstowe – where she spent the whole afternoon shopping in the January sales. She didn't even go inside the house.'

'We can check with Atherton and Khan,' Emily added, 'but it sounds as if she wasn't on her own with the samples at any point before she went out.'

Jack kicked a stone and watched it skitter down the road. This was absurd! Surely they hadn't lost their prime suspect *again*? 'Margaret must be lying!' he insisted. 'She could have just pretended to go out shopping. Maybe she sneaked back and switched the samples?'

'Possibly,' Emily admitted. 'But we'd need a lot more proof than a missing mammoth rib before we accuse her.'

'Especially with our track record in this investigation!' Scott laughed. 'We've already got it wrong twice. And apart from anything else, it'll be World War Three with Harry Atherton if he thinks Margaret is the one who's been messing up his research! It'd be like the time Jack went on my computer and sent me back fifteen levels on World of Warcraft.'

'That was an accident!' Jack protested.

'So *you* say!'

Emily gazed out to sea. A lone fishing boat was chugging its way back to shore. Scott had a point, she thought. Even if Margaret really *was* the culprit, maybe it would be better to keep quiet and not tell Harry?

But could it ever be right to hide the truth?

That's if they could ever find out what the truth *was*, of course!

Eighteen

Setting the Trap

Instead of heading back down to the village, the friends drifted aimlessly onto the headland and sat down on a bench to try to figure out their next move. The last scraps of snow had finally melted away and the sun was sparkling off the waves in Key Bay. Scott watched Drift stalk a group of seagulls squabbling over a chip wrapper. Only two more days and he and Jack would be going back to London.

He couldn't bear the thought of leaving Castle Key knowing that Driftosaurus would be destroyed. They *had* to find out who was trying to make the fossil look like a hoax and stop the diggers starting work at the quarry again.

The seagulls finally had enough of Drift and scattered. Silhouetted against the pale blue sky their wings formed curved black M-shapes as they soared above the cliffs. Something about those shapes suddenly made everything click into place in Scott's head. What if the M on the door of the security guard's van hadn't been an M at all, but a stylized image of a black bird in flight? A black bird such as a *raven*, for example! Maybe those rumours about Raven Resorts buying the quarry to build a theme park weren't so far-fetched after all – and maybe the guard was working for them! But before Scott could tell Jack and Emily about his brainwave, they began shushing him and pointing at the Trago Art Gallery nearby.

'Don't look now . . .' Emily whispered.

'It's the Kerrows!' Jack hissed.

Sure enough, Russ Kerrow was holding a ladder against the wall while Liam was at the top swabbing a row of tiny diamond-shaped windows.

Scott shrugged. What were Jack and Emily getting so agitated about? 'Oooh, window cleaners!' he gasped, pretending to be shocked. 'And they're *cleaning windows*! Whatever next!'

Emily rolled her eyes. 'The Kerrows were at Coastguard Cottage on Saturday.'

'So what?' Scott asked.

'The Kerrows were working up on the dome,' Jack said. 'If Margaret really went straight out to the shops like she said, they'd have seen her. Or, if she drove off and then sneaked back to the house to change the samples . . .'

'They're key witnesses,' Emily spelled out. 'We have to interview them immediately.'

Scott realized they had a point. His brainwave about the M-that-might-really-be-a-raven could wait until later. Together they headed to the gallery to talk to Russ Kerrow.

After a long discussion of the weather and the highs and lows of the window-cleaning life, they finally worked the conversation around to the glass dome at Coastguard Cottage and then to the dinosaur fossil. 'We're trying to figure out whether anyone could have broken into the house on Saturday,' Emily said. 'Did you see anything unusual?'

Russ Kerrow chewed on his cigarette. 'I don't think so. We were there all afternoon. Snow leaves terrible streaks on the glass, you know.'

'Did you see Margaret Atherton go out in the car at all?' Scott asked.

Russ Kerrow frowned so hard his deep-set eyes disappeared into nests of wrinkles. 'Oh, yes, that's right,' he said eventually. 'She shouted up and asked if we needed anything in town.'

'I bet she stopped and doubled back though?' Jack prompted, unable to hide his eagerness to prove that Margaret was the sample-swapper.

Kerrow gave him a blank look, but Liam was suddenly scooting down the ladder to join them.

'Yeah, I saw her come back,' he said, wiping his soapy hands down his overalls. 'She stopped the jeep at the bottom of the drive and ran to the back door. She must have forgotten something.'

Scott could barely hide his surprise. It seemed Jack had been right all along. Margaret had sneaked back and switched the samples! Meanwhile Emily was gazing at Liam Kerrow with an odd faraway look on her face. It looked as if Jack was right about something else as well: Emily *did* have a crush on Liam Kerrow! Scott didn't know what she saw in him. Kerrow had one of those half-starved vampire faces – all black hair, piercing eyes and cheekbones – that girls seemed to go mad over . . .

As they left the Kerrows to get on with their work, Jack grinned. 'Was I was right or was I right? I told you Margaret was lying.'

But Emily didn't reply. Suddenly she turned and called back to Liam Kerrow. 'You said Margaret *ran* back to the house. She must have been limping, with that bad ankle of hers?'

Scott was about to correct Emily – it was Professor Khan who had the twisted ankle, not Margaret Atherton – when he realized that Emily was Up to Something. Maybe it wasn't Liam's cheekbones she was interested in after all.

'Oh, er, yeah, that's right,' Liam shouted from the ladder. 'She was definitely hobbling. She might have had a stick, now I think about it.'

'I don't get it,' Jack whispered. 'Why was Margaret limping?'

'That's the point. She *wasn't*!' Emily explained, as they sat back down on the bench. 'I just said it to test Liam because I suspected he was inventing that whole story about Margaret returning to the house. Nobody remembers a detail from two days ago *that* fast. I was watching his face. He didn't think about it for a second.'

'And I thought you were just staring into his eyes because you fancied him!' Jack laughed.

'So immature!' Scott snorted. He wasn't going to admit he'd been thinking the exact same thing!

'But why would Liam tell a random lie like that?' Jack asked.

Emily jumped up from the bench with such a manic gleam in her eyes that Jack thought she was about to punch him for teasing her about Liam. But Emily only slapped *herself* on the forehead. 'Because it's not random! Liam was at Coastguard Cottage both times the dinosaur samples were switched!'

'No, he wasn't,' Scott said. 'We've been through this before, remember? They left Coastguard Cottage before we brought back the first batch of samples so we ruled them out.'

Emily gave an apologetic grin. 'I know. That's what I thought. But I've just realized I got it wrong. I can't believe I was so blind!'

Jack did a double take. Was Emily hallucinating or something? They'd definitely watched from the Land Rover as the Kerrows loaded their van. 'We saw them leave with our own eyes!'

Emily shook her head. 'We saw *Russ* Kerrow leave.'

Jack replayed the scene in his mind: Russ Kerrow single-handedly fighting off the reporters who were trying to grab his ladder. Of course! *Single-handedly* was the operative word. 'So where was Liam then?'

'He must have gone back into the house,' Emily said. 'I think he heard us talking with Professor Khan and Melvin Spencer about going to get samples when he came to deliver that message from his Dad about packing up for the day. He'd probably been lurking outside Atherton's lab for some time. Then he came up with the idea of making the dinosaur look like a hoax so, instead of leaving with his dad, he made up some excuse to stay and then stole back inside. He snapped a bit of bone off Ivan and waited for us to come back so he could switch the samples!' At last Emily paused for breath.

'Hang on a minute!' Jack interrupted. 'How did Liam get back inside Coastguard Cottage? Margaret double-checked all the doors and windows were locked.'

Emily frowned. 'What if he found a hiding place inside the house before we went out? Maybe Margaret locked him in rather than out!'

The moment he heard the words 'hiding place' Jack knew Emily was right. 'The Mundimba grain basket!' he exclaimed.

Emily and Scott stared at him as if he'd gone mad.

'That massive basket by the front door! That must be where Liam hid.'

'Of course!' Scott agreed. 'We thought that the thudding noises we heard when we came up from the kitchen to escape from the sprout soup were Melvin Spencer on his way back from the loo, but it must have been Liam knocking the basket over as he made a speedy getaway after swapping the samples. I bet he couldn't believe his luck when The Raspberry left them right there in the hall.'

'We must have missed him by seconds!' Emily groaned. 'We'd have noticed his footprints leading away from the front door if the snow around the house hadn't already been churned up by the reporters. Another lucky break for Liam!'

Emily leaned back on the bench and closed her eyes. Even those weird chemicals that had turned up on the fossil samples made sense now. Glue from the mammoth bones. Window-cleaning detergent from Liam Kerrow's hands. All the pieces were falling into place. Well, all except one: the minor detail of a *motive*.

Scott was clearly thinking the same thing. 'But why would Liam want to go to all that trouble to make the megalosaurus fossil look like a fake?' he asked.

Emily shrugged. 'Well, we've ruled out everyone else who had access to the samples. And he was definitely lying about Margaret too. There *has* to be a motive somewhere. Probably one of the big three: jealousy, revenge or money . . .'

'Or passion!' Jack chipped in. 'Maybe old Liam's in l-u-u-u-r-ve with Professor Khan!'

Scott rolled his eyes. 'Have you been reading that soppy Tristan and Iseult stuff again?'

'We'll just have to work out the motive later,' Emily said, jumping up off the bench. 'First we need hard evidence to *prove* Liam's the culprit.'

'And we need it fast,' Scott added. 'A couple more days and the diggers will be back.'

'If only we could force Kerrow into giving himself away,' Emily murmured, thinking aloud.

They all fell silent. That wasn't going to be easy.

Suddenly, Scott's face lit up. 'I've got a plan,' he announced.

Moments later, the friends sauntered past the Trago Gallery as if heading back down to the village. When they were close to Liam Kerrow's ladder, Scott dialled Emily's number, keeping his phone hidden in his pocket. Emily's ring tone – the James Bond theme tune – blared out at top volume.

Emily took out her phone as if answering the call. 'It's Professor Atherton,' she announced loudly to the boys. 'Ooh, brilliant! He says they've just got some really good results from the latest test. Evidence that our dinosaur is *definitely* genuine.' Then she spoke into the phone. 'Yes, Professor Atherton, we'll come to the lab now.'

'At last!' Jack yelled, just in case Liam Kerrow hadn't quite got the message. 'Proof that the dinosaur isn't a hoax after all!'

With the trap set, the three friends and Drift hurried down the hill. But at the first bend in the road they ducked down behind a crumbling stone wall. Emily pulled her binoculars from her bag and looked back up the headland towards the Trago Gallery. 'It's working!' she breathed. She watched Liam Kerrow scramble down the ladder, exchange a few words with his father and then jog towards the red van. He'd pulled a mobile phone from his pocket and was dialling as he got in behind the wheel.

'Result!' Jack said, high-fiving Scott and Emily. 'Kerrow has taken the bait. He's racing off to find this new "proof" and destroy it.'

'Hurry up,' Scott urged. 'We've got to follow him to Coastguard Cottage and catch him in the act!' They started to run up the hill, but they all stopped and stared as the van pulled onto the coast road. Instead of turning left and heading east towards Coastguard Cottage, Kerrow turned right.

He was driving back towards Castle Key village.

Nineteen

Run!

The friends scurried back behind the wall as Kerrow drove past.

'That wasn't supposed to happen,' Jack said. 'Where's he going?'

Emily didn't know. But she'd already lost three prime suspects in Operation Dinosaur: Liam Kerrow wasn't going to get away that easily. She sprinted down the hill, Drift bounding along behind her. 'Come on,' she called over her shoulder.

As they ran into the square, Emily saw the red van parked on the kerb. 'Eyeball on target's wheels!' she muttered, pulling the boys out of sight behind a sign that announced that a jumble sale was about to start in the village hall.

'Target has flown!' Emily breathed, scanning the square. Where could Kerrow have gone? The village hall? The church? Neither jumble nor prayers seemed likely. The pub? Of course! Kerrow must have phoned an accomplice and arranged to meet at the Ship and Anchor.

The friends crept down the alley that ran alongside the old whitewashed pub to the delivery entrance at the back. A white van was parked behind the brewery lorry. Close up, a small black shape could be seen on the door.

'The security guard!' Jack, Scott and Emily whispered in perfect unison.

'And I was right.' Scott pointed at the motif, which he now saw was very clearly a black bird with outstretched wings. 'It's a raven.'

'Make your mind up! You said it was an M,' Jack objected. 'You never said anything about *ravens*!'

But Emily was staring at Scott, her eyes as wide as frisbees. 'Of course! The guard works for Raven Resorts.'

Jack shrugged. 'It's a bit of a coincidence that he's suddenly popped up again now.'

Emily grabbed Jack's arm. 'That's it! It's *not* a coincidence. Liam and the security guard *know* each other.'

'How d'you figure that out?' Scott asked.

'It was when the Kerrows gave us a lift the other day. I knew something Liam said didn't add up. I just couldn't put my finger on what it was – until now. He said someone could go in the front because it was squashed in the back with *Tyson and Rambo.*'

'And your point is?' Jack asked.

Emily groaned with impatience. 'How did he know what the dogs were called? We definitely didn't say their names as we got in.'

Scott caught on. 'Liam must have met Rambo and Tyson before.'

'That's right. So, Liam is linked to the security guard, which means he's also linked to Raven Resorts.' Emily spoke slowly, trying to keep her excitement in check. She sensed they were only a breath away from finding Liam's motive and solving the mystery of the dinosaur hoax.

The three friends edged to the pub window and peeped inside. The ancient glass was thick and whorled, but Emily could make out two men sitting in a dark alcove beyond the roaring fire. One was Liam Kerrow. The other man was hidden in the shadows. He leaned forward to pick up his pint. Emily was straining to see when a sudden outbreak of barking made her jump so violently she banged her nose on the glass. She looked down for Drift, who had been sitting patiently at her feet just moments before. He was gone.

Following the noise, Emily ran to the front of the pub. There was Drift, gleefully greeting Tyson and Rambo, who were tethered by their leads to a hook inside the porch.

'Shhh, Drift! You'll give us away!' Emily hissed.

But it was too late. The door of the Ship and Anchor flew open and Emily found herself staring straight up at the guard's beefy red face. Liam Kerrow was right behind him.

'I told you those kids were asking too many questions!' Kerrow spat.

'Well, I'll soon teach them not stick their noses in!' the guard shouted, making a grab for Emily.

Emily jumped back. She caught her foot in one of the dogs' leads and stumbled, but Scott and Jack were right behind her. They caught her by the arms and pulled her out of reach.

'Run!' Jack yelled.

Emily just had time to glimpse the flash of rage in the guard's bulging eyes before she turned and tore across the square, closely followed by Scott, Jack, Drift, Tyson, Rambo and the two men. She didn't know what the guard would do if he caught them, but she was pretty sure his style of 'teaching' didn't involve multiple choice questions or spelling tests – and she wasn't going to hang around to find out.

'Down here!' she hissed. Scott and Jack flew after her into a narrow alley between the village hall and the scout hut.

At that precise moment, Mrs Loveday stepped into the alley wheeling a rack of old clothes destined for the jumble sale. Emily, Scott and the dogs dodged her, but Jack only avoided knocking her down like a skittle by grabbing her round the waist and spinning her to one side, like something out of *Strictly Come Dancing*.

'Hoodlum!' Mrs Loveday screeched.

'Sorry!' Jack yelled, darting away. Then he had an idea. He turned back, seized the clothes rack and rolled it towards Kerrow and the guard, who were barrelling down the alley behind him. They hit the rack at full tilt and keeled over. *Yes!* Jack thought. *That was just like a chase scene in a movie.* But he didn't have time to admire the effect for long. The two men were already extracting themselves from the tangle of hand-knitted jumpers and flowery skirts. Jack turned and ran to catch up with Scott and Emily.

As the friends raced along the seafront Kerrow and the guard were gaining on them again. They bolted up Sprat Lane and zig-zagged through the maze of old cottages behind Dotty's Tea Rooms, finally coming out in Fish Alley.

'In here!' Emily panted, darting through a side door.

'What *is* this place?' Jack puffed, gazing around a gloomy, echoing warehouse. There were enormous weighing scales along one side and stacks of red-and-blue plastic crates reached almost to the ceiling.

'The fish market,' Emily said. 'It's closed today.'

Jack shivered. He had a feeling that if the security guard got his way, it wouldn't just be fish hanging up by the gills from the gleaming metal hooks on the walls.

'We can get out the back!' Emily sprinted to a door in the far corner. She seized the handle. She pulled. Then she pushed. Nothing happened.

The door was locked.

Twenty

A Job for the Canine Division

The men were right behind them now. Emily could hear their footsteps slapping on the wet concrete floor. She rattled the handle in frustration. *They were trapped!* She knew she had to do something fast. She whispered urgently to Drift. 'Distraction! Runaway!' Then she threw herself behind a walk-in freezer with the boys and held her breath. Two commands together was asking a lot of Drift. Could he remember them both and pull it off?

Drift pricked up his brown spotted ear. *Distraction?* He loved this command! All he had to do was cause maximum disruption. And he had a great idea. He alerted Tyson and Rambo with a short yip, then lowered his head and charged. The Dobermans exchanged confused looks, but then dutifully copied their hero. *Bam! Bam! Bam!* The three dogs torpedoed into a tower of crates. The crates wobbled, then toppled over, crashing down on Kerrow and the guard in an avalanche of brightly coloured plastic. Drift nudged noses – the canine version of a high-five – with Tyson and Rambo. But then he remembered Emily had given him a *second* command. What was it? Play Dead? No, it was Runaway! Woofing for Tyson and Rambo to follow, Drift darted out of the door.

Meanwhile, the two men were clambering out from beneath the crates. The guard brushed a fish head from his shoulder. 'Just wait till I get my hands on those kids!' he raged, staring wildly around the warehouse.

Behind the freezer, Emily's stomach was curdling with fear. But just when she thought they were sure to be found, Kerrow caught sight of the dogs disappearing out of the door where they'd originally come in.

'This way!' he shouted. And with that the two men were gone.

'Phew, that was a close one!' Jack whispered as the

friends crawled out from their hiding place. 'I thought we were fishfingers for a minute there!'

'Drift really saved the day this time,' Scott said. 'I hope he's alright.'

Emily glowed with pride. She knew Drift would be fine. He would lead the men on a long chase round the village and only double back when he was sure it was safe.

As they made for the door, Scott noticed a mobile phone lying on the concrete. He picked it up, wiped off the fish slime and opened the Settings screen. 'It's registered to Liam Kerrow. He must have dropped it when the crates hit him.'

'Wow! There'll be all kinds of brilliant clues on there!' Emily was so excited, she forgot her manners. She snatched the phone, clicked onto Recent Calls and quickly scrolled back to the day they'd gone with Professor Atherton and Professor Khan to collect the first batch of fossil samples. 'What time was it when we set off for the quarry in Margaret's Land Rover?' she asked.

Jack was used to Emily's bizarre questions by now. They usually made sense if you waited long enough. 'Late morning. About time for elevenses. Why?'

Emily looked up from the phone's display with a triumphant gleam in her eyes. 'This must be it,' she breathed. 'A phone call made at eleven thirty that morning. I bet a million pounds this was Liam phoning

Raven Resorts. When he heard us talking about the dinosaur, he must have realized straight away that a mega-important dinosaur find at the quarry would mess up Raven's plans to build the theme park. So he got on the phone and offered to switch the samples to make it look like a fake – for a hefty price, no doubt.'

Scott grinned. 'I said at the start of this investigation that Raven Resorts might have paid Professor Khan to set up the hoax for them. I was right all along.'

'Excuse me!' Jack chimed in. 'But it was Liam Kerrow, not Nadira Khan. In what sense does that make you *right*?'

'OK, I got the wrong *person*. But I was right about the reason.'

'Well, we can soon find out!' Jack reached for the phone and clicked on the mystery number before the others could stop him.

'Raven Resorts. How can I help you?'

The three friends stared at each other. They were right!

'Raven Resorts. Is anyone there?'

'Sorry, wrong number,' Jack mumbled, hanging up.

'Looks like Liam Kerrow is one prime suspect who *isn't* going to wriggle off the hook,' Emily said happily as she slipped the phone inside a small evidence bag in her satchel.

'Talking of wriggling off hooks, let's get out of here,' Jack laughed. 'This place stinks of fish guts.'

As they left the warehouse, Scott was feeling very pleased with himself. The trap to catch Liam Kerrow had worked perfectly – if not exactly how he'd planned. And now, with the phone, they had all the evidence they needed to hand over the case to D. I. Hassan. The only question was how Liam knew that Raven Resorts were planning to build on the quarry, when everyone else – including Emily – had thought it was just a rumour . . .

Blinking in the sunlight after the gloom of the fish market, the friends saw Drift trotting along the alley towards them. From the jaunty wag of his tail, it was clear he'd managed to get Kerrow and the guard well and truly lost. They all hugged him for his heroic work. To Jack's disappointment Tyson and Rambo were nowhere to be seen. The security guard must have caught them again.

'Let's go to Dotty's and order Drift a whole pizza to himself as a reward!' Jack suggested. 'With extra ham.'

Drift's ears pricked up. *Ham* was one of his favourite words!

But he never did get his pizza. They were about to enter the café when a purple camper van came speeding along the seafront. A voice blared out from a megaphone poking through the sun roof.

'SAVE OUR DRAGON NOW!'

Twenty-one

The Call to Battle

The camper van lurched to a halt along with several other vehicles from the camp on the common and Graham Fothergill's truck. They were all sounding their horns, as if this were a carnival procession through downtown Rio.

Izzy leaned down from the top of the camper van, her blonde dreads bouncing around her face. 'THEY'VE STARTED WORK UP AT THE QUARRY!' she boomed. Then she lowered the megaphone. 'We've got to stop them.'

Emily shook her head. 'That can't be right. The council called Professor Atherton this morning and told him that Trimble and Sons wouldn't start work until next week!'

Skye's head appeared from the driver's side window. 'Trimble doesn't own the quarry any more. Turns out this company called Raven Resorts has bought the site on the quiet!'

'THEY'RE DESTROYING OUR CORNISH DRAGON!' Izzy proclaimed through the megaphone.

'STANDING IN THE WAY OF SCIENTIFIC INVESTIGATION!' Graham had rigged up some kind of amplifier system on the back of his truck and seemed to be competing with Izzy to make the most noise.

'Are you sure it's Raven?' Scott asked.

Skye nodded. 'We just got the tip-off from a journalist friend in Bristol. She's been investigating Charlie Raven for years.' She clapped her hands over her ears as Graham's amplifier squealed with feedback. 'Raven has secretly bought the land. He's got permission to start levelling it already because he's convinced the council that the fossil's a hoax. We're rounding up as many supporters as we can to stop them destroying the dragon with their diggers.'

'IT'S A GOVERNMENT COVER-UP TO KEEP THE ALIEN LIZARDS SECRET!' Molly Dunnock had wrestled Graham's microphone from him, and was now addressing the small crowd of onlookers who'd gathered to see what all the commotion was about.

'DOWN WITH THE DRAGON KILLERS!' Izzy bellowed, not to be outdone.

There was a chorus of horns from the vehicles behind.

'Got to go!' Skye shouted, grinding the camper van into gear.

'We're coming with you!' Jack yanked open the back door. 'We've got to save Driftosaurus!'

Emily piled in after him with Scott and Drift. But as they began to pull away she looked through the window and noticed her dad coming out of Dotty's with a takeaway coffee and a bemused look on his face. 'Wait!' she cried, jumping out of the van and into his path.

Seth Wild tugged at his grey ponytail, trying to work out how his daughter had suddenly appeared out of thin air.

'Dad!' Emily gasped. 'You've got to get everyone in HOCKI up to the quarry before it's too late.'

'Whoah! Slow down there!' Seth Wild sipped his coffee. He wasn't a guy to rush into things. 'Now, what's this all about?'

'Dad! *Now!*' Emily yelled. She could hear Skye revving the camper van impatiently.

'RAVEN RESORTS MUST BE STOPPED!' Izzy shouted.

'Raven Resorts?' Dad echoed. 'I *knew* it! Well, we won't stand by while they turn our island into a theme park! Leave it with me!'

Emily flashed him a thumbs-up and clambered back into the van. 'You can take the short cut up Church Lane and along the cart track,' she told Skye. Skye put her foot down and they roared out of the village at the head of the convoy.

'I've called D. I. Hassan to tell him what's happening,' Scott said. 'Atherton and Khan too. They'll meet us there.'

By the time the camper van had bounced over the moor and rammed the quarry fence, Jack felt as if his brain had rattled loose. But when he ran up the slope he realized that a wobbly brain was the least of his worries. Two bulldozers and a colossal yellow digger were roaring their way towards Driftosaurus. The tarpaulin cover flapped forlornly in the breeze. It was hardly going to protect the ancient Jurassic giant from these twenty-first century predators.

'Form a circle round the dragon!' Skye commanded.

Jack, Scott and Emily found themselves joining hands and chanting 'We shall not be moved' along with all the others. Drift joined in by standing in the middle of the ring, barking in time.

'Look!' Scott shouted, freeing his hand from Izzy's grip and pointing to a gleaming black Jaguar that was rolling up to the quarry gates. A broad-shouldered man in a pin-striped suit strode towards them, shouting into a mobile phone and waving a cigar.

'That must be Charlie Raven,' Emily cried.

'Lizard hater!' Molly Donnock screamed at him.

The machines were only metres away from the dinosaur fossil now, but suddenly the digger stopped and then the bulldozers.

Everyone cheered.

But their celebrations came too soon.

'What are you stopping for?' Raven bellowed at the drivers. 'It's just a bunch of kids and hippies! They'll soon scarper when they see we mean business.'

The vehicles started up again. *There's no way they'd actually drive right over us,* Scott told himself. But the digger was so close now that he could see worms dangling from clods of earth on the shovel. He began to back away, but suddenly Izzy dived headfirst on top of Driftosaurus, dragging Scott with her. Within seconds, the entire circle of protestors had hit the deck like a row of dominoes.

Scott lay spread-eagled with a fossilized horn digging into his ribs. He felt the earth beneath him vibrate under the heavy machinery, as if the megalosaurus was shaking itself awake after a hundred-million-year sleep. *If only!* Scott thought. *There's* really *no way they'd actually drive right over us,* he told himself again – although this time with far less conviction. Charlie Raven didn't look like the kind of guy to back down.

I can't believe it, Jack thought. *I'm risking my life to save something that's already been dead for a hundred million years!* But he didn't move.

Nor did Emily. This was her investigation. No way was

she going to let Raven and Kerrow win! She tried to push Drift out of harm's way but he refused to move from her side so she clung to him and buried her face in his fur.

Jack closed his eyes. Aunt Kate had been right all along. The quarry was dangerous. *If we hadn't gone through the fence we'd never have found the fossil and we wouldn't be about to be pulverized . . .*

The smell of oil and earth filled his nostrils.

Was this really it? *Game over?*

'EMILY!'

The voice came from behind him. Jack looked over his shoulder to see Emily flying through the air. Seth Wild had grabbed his daughter and, with superhuman strength, thrown her out of the path of the oncoming bulldozer. Then he raised his hands. With his long grey hair flying free of his ponytail he looked like Moses about to part the Red Sea. 'Stop!' he yelled at the machine drivers.

Charlie Raven shoved him aside. 'Don't stop, you idiots! *Go!*'

But Emily's dad had now been joined by a huge crowd, streaming up the slope and brandishing placards saying HANDS OFF! and RAVEN RESORTS OUT!

The drivers turned off their engines. It was clear they weren't prepared to mow down half the population of the island.

Emily's mum stepped out from the crowd, punched Raven on the nose, then scooped Emily up in her arms.

Everyone cheered.

Jack watched in a daze as Scott stood up, calmly retrieved Graham's tin foil hat from the digger's shovel, straightened it out and handed it to him. Jack had to admit, that was a pretty cool move – if you hadn't seen the look of blind terror on Scott's face just moments before!

All at once everyone was laughing and high-fiving and congratulating each other for putting a stop to Raven's plan. Harry and Margaret Atherton and Professor Khan arrived and started explaining the importance of the megalosaurus fossil to anyone who would listen.

Emily was still hugging her parents – secretly *very* relieved not to have been crushed under a bulldozer – when Drift ran off barking joyfully. He bounded back moments later with Rambo and Tyson in tow.

That means the security guard is here somewhere, Emily realized. Operation Dinosaur wasn't over yet and there was work to do! She dodged her mum's hugs, found the boys and together they ran to look for the white van. But, instead, they found a red van with ladders on top, drawing up near the quarry gates.

'It's Liam Kerrow!' Jack shouted.

Kerrow opened the door. When he saw Jack, Scott and Emily his face twisted with anger. Then he caught sight of the crowd of Castle Key residents – including his father, waving a NO TO RAVEN banner – and he turned to climb back into the van. But he was blocked by a three-pronged flying ambush from Drift, Tyson and Rambo.

For one terrible moment, Jack thought the dogs were

tearing Kerrow to pieces, but then he saw that their tails were wagging and they were snuffling around like airport sniffer dogs who'd just detected a suitcase full of drugs. Drift hopped up behind Kerrow onto the seat of the van. When he reappeared a moment later, it wasn't drugs he held between his teeth, but an enormous bone.

Jack did a double take. 'That's Ivan's rib!' he shouted.

'What are you talking about?' Kerrow blustered, his eyes flicking nervously around the crowd. 'It's just a butcher's bone I brought to give my mate for his dogs. He's here somewhere. He'll tell you.' He looked around, but it seemed that the guard had made himself scarce.

Emily called Drift and asked him to hand over the bone. Rather reluctantly, the little dog dropped it at her feet. Professor Khan stepped forward, took the bone from Emily and held it up to the light. Then she smiled at Liam Kerrow. 'And your butcher *regularly* stocks prehistoric woolly-mammoth bones, does he?'

Russ Kerrow stared at his son, slowly shaking his head. He opened his mouth and his cigarette fell to the ground. 'Liam. What have you done?'

Liam hesitated for a moment. Then he dived back into his van, gunned the engine and drove off with the door flapping open and a squeal of tyres.

At least he *would* have driven off, if he hadn't been surrounded by the high-speed arrival of three police cars with flashing blue lights and wailing sirens.

Twenty-two

A Full Case Report

The following afternoon, Scott, Jack, Emily and Drift gathered in the kitchen at Coastguard Cottage. In addition to Margaret and Harry Atherton, Detective Inspector Hassan was also present; he'd arranged the meeting to go through a few questions about the dinosaur hoax.

Emily slid a bulging file of typed notes across the table. 'This is a full case report,' she told D. I. Hassan.

'It explains exactly how Liam Kerrow switched the two sets of samples from the megalosuarus fossil, with bone fragments from the woolly mammoth in the tower room to make the dinosaur look like a fake. I think you'll find all the evidence you need. I've included a set of fingerprints taken from the big basket in the hall where he hid . . .'

'The Mundimba grain basket,' Jack clarified.

Margaret Atherton shot him a delighted smile.

Emily continued without missing a beat. 'And I'm quite sure those chemical traces in the fossil samples will match the detergents the Kerrows use for window cleaning, plus Liam's hair gel, and the glue from Ivan's skeleton . . .'

'Oh, and here's Kerrow's mobile phone,' Scott added, placing the evidence bag on top of the file. You'll find the numbers for Raven Resorts and the security guard under Recent Calls.'

D. I. Hassan's eyebrows twitched as he examined the phone and flicked through the pages of notes. 'Very thorough, I must say.' He sipped his coffee, then smoothed down his moustache – which looked blacker and glossier than ever. 'In fact, Liam Kerrow has already made a full confession. It seems that when he first heard you three talking with Professor Atherton about the dinosaur find, he immediately realized that he could turn it to his advantage and make some money from the situation. He called Charlie Raven and offered to set up the "hoax" in return for a large sum of money and the contract for cleaning all the windows of the new hotel complex when it was built. Kerrow then told his father that Margaret Atherton had asked him to stay on and do some odd jobs at Coastguard Cottage, and hid inside the house . . .'

'In the Mundimba grain basket,' Scott and Emily chorused, grinning at Jack.

D. I. Hassan stopped short, suddenly realizing he was giving away too much information. 'Obviously, I can't reveal any further details at this point.'

Scott nodded seriously. 'Just one question. Or, rather, two! How come Liam Kerrow had the number for Raven Resorts? And how did he know they'd bought the quarry site?'

'I shouldn't tell you any more,' D. I. Hassan said, but then he tapped the file. 'But as you've been so generous with your information, I'll just say that Charlie Raven's son, Nick, is a student in Bristol.'

Jack frowned. 'Er, yeah, that explains everything! *Not!*' he added, under his breath.

But Emily smiled. 'Of course! Liam went to college in Bristol last year. He must have made friends with Nick Raven there.'

'And of course,' Scott said casually, 'Charlie Raven sent one of his henchmen to pose as a security guard at the quarry, to keep an eye on Kerrow and make sure he kept his end of the bargain.'

'Yes, and to see that nobody was asking too many questions. He goes by the name of Joe King. Nasty piece of work.' D. I. Hassan suddenly realized that Scott had led him into giving away information yet again and fell silent.

An unwelcome memory of very nearly being filleted by Joe King in the fish market popped into Jack's mind. 'Did you catch him?' he asked nervously.

Hassan nodded. 'We intercepted him trying to leave the island by boat last night. He's already given us some very useful information about Raven Resorts' business practices. Charlie Raven has been bribing council officials to grant planning permission and to keep his plans secret.'

So that's *why I couldn't uncover any evidence that Raven was planning to build on the island when I looked into it for Dad last year,* Emily thought. *He's been paying people off to keep it all hush-hush!* She sighed with relief. For a moment she'd thought she had been losing her touch!

But Jack was worried about a different problem. 'If this King guy's in custody, what's happened to Tyson and Rambo?'

D. I. Hassan's moustache twitched. 'Tyson and Rambo?'

'His dogs,' Jack explained.

'Oh, yes. I believe that they are currently at the animal shelter in Carrickstowe waiting to be re-homed.'

Jack looked at Scott with hopeful puppy-eyes. *Maybe, just maybe . . .*

But Scott shook his head. 'Dad would never let us. And it wouldn't be fair to keep them cooped up in our little flat in London.'

Suddenly Emily jumped up. 'Wait! I've got a brilliant idea!' She grabbed her phone and ran outside into the corridor. Moments later she came back with a huge grin on her face. 'It's all sorted! I called Vicky White at Roshendra Farm. They've got loads of dogs there and she said two more would be no problem. We'll be able to see them any time we want!'

Jack swallowed a lump in his throat. He knew Scott and Emily were right. Tyson and Rambo would be much happier on the farm than in London.

'And maybe they can help us on investigations sometimes,' Scott said. 'Drift seems to have been training them up pretty well!'

Drift looked up from under the table where he was busy with a bone – definitely *not* one of Ivan's – that Margaret Atherton had given him, and wagged his tail happily.

━

Once D. I. Hassan had left, Professor Atherton turned his wheelchair to the friends and beamed. 'Now all we need to do is collect a new set of samples and start our tests again. I'm quite sure we'll find that the megalosaurus is genuine this time.' He chuckled. 'Even Nadira Khan is starting to believe me, so it must be true!'

The friends all laughed.

'Now, I have a surprise for you,' Atherton went on. He pressed several buttons on his control pad with his chin and the horizontal screen shot out from the side of the wheelchair. The 3D hologram of Driftosaurus came into view, rotating to show its fearsome jaws and claws and horns and spikes.

'Er, it's great!' Jack said, a little disappointed that the surprise wasn't anything new. 'But you did show us this before.'

Atherton pressed another button. Above the image a title emerged in huge capital letters: MEGAMEGALOSAURUS DRIFTII.

The three friends stared at the words.

'What do you think?' Margaret Atherton asked. '*Driftii*,' she pronounced it as Drift-eye, 'is the Latin way of forming the scientific name. This is what Harry will register the fossil as. It won't be official until it's all been verified and approved, of course.'

'Wow. That's mega!' Jack whistled.

'*Mega*-mega!' Scott laughed.

Emily cuddled her little dog on her lap. 'You're going to be famous, Drift!'

'Well, it's only right that the name of the discoverer

should be properly recognized!' Atherton said. 'Now, I need to get back up to the observatory to prepare for viewing tonight. Maggie, have you fixed that stairlift yet?'

'I told you. I did it this morning. You're going deaf in your old age!'

Harry Atherton zoomed towards the door but suddenly he spun the wheelchair round. 'I don't suppose you three would be interested in observing comet Messerspitze with me? It's in the process of exploding. Pretty spectacular! You'd have to stay up all night, of course.'

Jack grinned at the others. *An exploding comet? Staying up all night? You bet we're interested!*

'Yes, please!' they all said in unison.

'Then why don't you stay for a celebratory dinner first?' Margaret offered. 'It's the least we can do to thank you for all your help.'

Jack's heart sank. Oh, no. If Brussels sprout soup was on the menu again, how was he going to get out of it this time?

'I know, Maggie,' Atherton suddenly shouted. 'Why don't you make one of your famous Mexican feasts?'

Margaret smiled. 'Good idea! Chicken tortillas, spicy fajitas, salsas . . . how does all that sound?'

'Perfect!' Jack laughed. He shot Harry Atherton a grateful look. Maybe one of the gadgets on that wheelchair was a mind-reading device. Or perhaps

Harry just wasn't that keen on his sister's Brussels sprout soup either!

———

As they helped set the table for dinner, Scott suddenly remembered it was the last day of the holidays. Tomorrow he and Jack would be on the early train back to London, and Emily had school. 'Maybe staying up all night isn't such a sensible idea?' he suggested.

Jack stared at his brother in disbelief. 'I've always thought that *sensible* was seriously over-rated,' he said. 'And sleep, for that matter!'

Emily agreed. 'Yeah, and watching comets *is* highly educational.'

Scott thought about it for a moment. Then he grinned. Jack and Emily were right. There were far too many adventures to be had in Castle Key to waste time sleeping!

'We can always sleep on the train!' he laughed.

Author's Note

Megalosaurus is a genuine dinosaur. It was one of the earliest to be identified from fossilized bones. Fossilized footprints thought to belong to this species really have been found in a quarry near Oxford, but Megamegalosaurus Driftii *was invented for the purposes of this story. No megalosaurus fossils have been found in Cornwall – yet!*

The Mundimba grain basket, and the legend of Tristan and Iseult are also real, but the Messerspitze is a fictional comet.

Don't miss the next exciting mystery
in the *Adventure Island* series

THE MYSTERY OF THE
DROWNING MAN

Available now!

Read on for a special preview of the first chapter.

One

Out of the Blue

Emily Wild lay on her stomach on the warm rock, her head propped up on her elbows, and gazed across the water towards the gap in the cliffs that circled Keyhole Cove, almost cutting it off from the open sea. The hidden cove on the south coast of Castle Key, guarded by a battalion of jagged rocks, was once the haunt of smugglers running brandy and tobacco to Cornwall. Now it was one of

Emily's favourite places on the island.

It was the first day of the Easter holidays. Her friends Scott and Jack Carter were back from London to stay with their Great-aunt Kate. Together they'd rowed her little boat *Gemini* all the way to the cove and had spent the morning swimming and exploring rock pools, before stopping to eat their picnic. Sunlight was sparkling off waves of the deepest blue.

Everything was perfect.

And yet . . .

Emily's little dog Drift nudged her chin with his nose. He could tell something was troubling her.

She scooped up a handful of the tiny shells that sprinkled the beach like silver glitter, let them run through her fingers, and sighed. 'I hope we don't get any mysteries to solve this holiday!'

Jack was so shocked he dropped his ham roll. The girl lounging on the rock next to him *looked* like Emily Wild: the same mad tangle of chocolate-coloured curls, the same dark eyes, the same skinny brown arms and legs. And yet, this *couldn't* be Emily. Emily *lived* for mysteries! Her pen was permanently poised over her notebook, itching to write *OPERATION X* (with a double underline, of course) and a long list of suspects.

Either this girl was an imposter or something was seriously wrong.

Scott clearly felt the same way. 'What are you on

about, Em?' He glanced up from under his floppy fringe. 'You're not *ill*, are you?'

No way! Jack thought. *Emily* couldn't be ill. She was as tough as those wild grasses that sprouted from the sand dunes.

Emily laughed. 'Of course not! It's just this stupid music festival Dad's organizing up at the castle. From tomorrow I have to help Mum with cleaning and cooking every day because we'll have loads of guests at The Lighthouse and Dad'll be so busy. Even if the crime of the century was committed right under my nose, I wouldn't have time to investigate . . .'

Relieved that Emily wasn't suffering from some obscure disease, Jack salvaged his roll and brushed off the sand. He stuffed one half in his mouth and threw the other in the air. Drift caught it neatly in his jaws. 'Is that all?' he laughed.

'We'll help with your jobs,' Scott offered.

Jack nodded in agreement – although secretly he planned to leave the helping-with-jobs part to his brother. It was Scott's idea, after all and this *was* meant to be a holiday. 'I bet Sherlock Holmes didn't have this problem,' he laughed. 'Sorry, Watson, old chap, you'll have to crack the case of the Hound of the Baskervilles on your own because I've got to polish the toilet paper.'

Emily grinned. 'Thanks, guys!' Scott and Jack could be infuriating at times, but they were the best friends she'd ever had – apart from Drift, of course! Recruiting them onto her investigations team when they'd first come to stay in Castle Key last summer had been one of her smartest moves ever. 'Not that I'm expecting a major case to suddenly pop up out of the blue,' she added, 'but you never know!'

'And anyway,' Scott said, watching Drift chase a crab into a rock pool, 'your dad's festival isn't stupid. It's cool. He's got some awesome bands lined up.' It always amazed Scott that Emily was so unimpressed that her father had been lead guitarist in the super-group, Panic Mode. To Emily, Seth Wild was just your average nice-but-mildly-embarrassing dad. But to Scott, who played guitar in a band, and loved all kinds of retro music, Seth Wild was as much a hero as Jimi Hendrix or Eric Clapton, even though he'd retired from the music business years ago. 'He's even got Splinter Planet coming!'

'Who are Splinter Planet when they're at home?' Jack asked, reaching into his backpack for his personal chocolate supplies.

'*Who are Splinter Planet?*' Scott spluttered. 'That's like asking who are the Beatles? They started out in the 1970s and had about a million number ones before they split up. This'll be their first live performance since they re-formed last year.'

Jack shrugged. 'The 1970s? That's *prehistoric*.'

Emily laughed. 'Yeah, that megalosaurus fossil we found in the quarry at Christmas was probably at all their gigs.'

Scott aimed a grape at the back of Emily's head. 'Ha ha! I know they're ancient but their stuff is classic. And you must have heard of their guitarist? Nick Dylan's a total *legend*!'

'Of course I've heard of Nick Dylan,' Emily said.

'See,' Scott told Jack. 'At least *Emily* knows something about rock history!'

Emily grinned. 'Actually I've only heard of him because he checked into The Lighthouse this morning.'

Scott's jaw dropped open. 'You're kidding. *Nick Dylan* is staying at The Lighthouse? *The* Nick Dylan?'

'Yeah. And the rest of Splinter Planet as well. Dad's friends with them all.'

'That. Is. So. Cool!' Scott breathed.

But Emily had suddenly remembered something much more interesting than guitar heroes. She jumped up and pulled Scott to his feet. 'Wait till you see this! Stand there and stretch your arm out. You need to hold something in your hand.'

Jack fished in the picnic bag and held out a forgotten banana.

Emily nodded. 'Just the thing!'

Jack watched, enthralled. Scott looked a prize wally standing there, arm out, clutching a banana, as if feeding an invisible chimpanzee. It was such a pity there was no one else around to witness the sight. Then Jack had a brainwave. He sneaked his new phone out of his backpack under cover of a huge bar of white chocolate.

Emily stepped back three paces. She took a deep breath and squared her shoulders. All of a sudden she was leaping and spinning, her leg whizzing through the air in a blur of speed.

Her foot made contact with the banana.

The banana flew out of Scott's hand.

Jack stared at Emily, who was calmly brushing sand from her t-shirt. Then he looked down at his phone. *Oh, yes!* He'd caught it all. This photo was priceless! He'd save it up for a moment when he needed some heavy-duty ammunition! 'Wow! Where did you learn that, Em? It was like something out of *The Matrix*!'

Emily grinned. 'I've been doing kick-boxing lessons. After that horrible security guard chased us during Operation Dinosaur I figured I needed to learn self-defence.'

'Yes, well, good idea,' Scott mumbled, trying to claw back some shreds of dignity. 'Of course, I could've blocked you if I'd known you were going to do a roundhouse kick.'

Jack laughed. 'That's the element of surprise! You don't give your enemies a five-minute warning.'

Scott swore to himself he would *never* let anything this uncool happen again. He would sign up for a crash course in martial arts the instant he got back to London.

Emily turned to Jack. 'You want to have a go?'

Jack lay back on the rock. Emily was scary enough as it was, even without a black belt in kick-boxing.

'Nah, you're OK. I never spar on a full stomach.' It was true, he *had* scarfed down rather more of that white chocolate than was strictly advisable in a single sitting.

Drift dropped the mangled banana at Scott's feet, eagerly waiting for him to launch it into orbit again. But suddenly the little dog pricked up his ears – first the black one, then the white one with brown spots. He dashed to the water's edge and barked at the waves.

The three friends sprinted into the shallows after him. When Drift's ears went into Listening Formation like this, he was never mistaken. And yet, there was not a sound to be heard above the constant crashing of the waves and the wailing of the seagulls.

Emily ran back to *Gemini* and grabbed her binoculars. She swept the expanse of water between the cliffs: nothing but dark patches of seaweed and gulls bobbing on the waves.

'What's that?' Jack cried, pointing towards the rocks where the cove narrowed. Scott shaded his eyes with his hand. 'It could be a seal . . .'

Suddenly Emily spotted the shape moving in the water.

She knew what a seal looked like.

It wasn't a seal.